A Sleuth in The Haven

a Gwen Harris Mystery

Carol Sheldon

Published by Houghton, 501 Via Casitas, Greenbrae CA 94904

All of the characters are fictitious, except Sally Stanford

OTHER NOVELS BY CAROL SHELDON

Mother Lode
Driven to Rage
A Sleuth in Sausalito
A Sleuth in the Summer of Love
Exposed: The Poetry of Carol Sheldon

CHILDREN'S BOOKS:
Penny's Christmas Tree
Craig's Crazy Cruise

Visit the author and her books at
Website/blog: www.carolsheldon.com

Cover Design courtesy of Denise Cassino

If you enjoy this book, why not get the others in the Gwen Harris Mystery Series? To order: amazon.com books by title or author.

It's Sausalito in the sixties. Poets, painters and philosophers dot this artsy town. After ten years of not knowing what happened to her mother when she disappeared, Gwen Harris is notified that recently discovered remains might be those of her mother. Gwen begins a long and arduous journey of discovering what happened, and who is responsible. Eager, but young and vulnerable, her trust in several people is shattered by secrecy, betrayal and deception.

As a columnist for the San Francisco Chronicle in 1967, Gwen Harris is supposed to just *report* on the phenomenon known as the Summer of Love, where peace and love are the mantras. But murder? Kidnapping? Gwen can't just stand by. In her efforts to discover the guilty and rescue the innocent, Gwen is caught in a web of events that threaten her love relationship, and eventually, even her life.

Acknowledgments

Many people contributed to the final version of this book The greatest was my editor and friend, Teresa LeYung Ryan, who spent countless hours giving me an overall critique, plus twelve short recordings of page to page comments, all the time keeping my spirits up by calling me brilliant. Next is my brother, David Sheldon, whose technical expertise helped enormously in preparing the print and e-book formats for publication. Others who gave valuable comments were Steve Olian, Wanda Henson and Roberta Malloy. Proof-readers included Mary Freeman, Becky Nichols and Joan Frentzel.

I wish to acknowledge the Bay Area Independent Publishing Association (BAIPA) for their years of encouragement to all authors who wish to publish independently, bringing invaluable lessons through speakers, panels and encouragement to its members.

CHAPTER 1

I am going to find you, Charlene. Have to. Lying on that pee-soaked mattress for thirty-five years, I had plenty of time to work out the details. And now I know your whereabouts. You're down by San Francisco in a town called San Rafael. Now I'm out. And it's payback time, sister mine.

~~~

Ignoring the alarm when it first went off, Gwen Harris was stunned when she opened one eye and saw the time.

Leaping out of bed, she dressed quickly, still pulling on her straight cotton skirt as she raced to the bathroom. *Of all days to be late!*

She splashed some water on her face, fastened her pony tail with a rubber band, and put on some Maybelline lipstick called Ripe Cherries. More attractive than beautiful, her most stunning feature was her green eyes.

She gulped down a cup of instant coffee, which her roommate Denise had made for her. This would give her a jump-start until she got to work at *The Chronicle*, where she'd enjoy a real cup of Joe.

"Today's the interview with your boss, right?"

"Right, and I don't want to be late."

"Well, good luck. Hope you get the position."

"Thanks."

Grabbing a piece of cold toast, she said goodbye to Denise, ran down the steps and got in her old VW. She was twenty-three years old, with a degree in journalism from the University of Michigan, Gwen had now been working for *The Chronicle* in San Francisco for six months. Today she had arranged an appointment with her boss. *I want to get the vacancy Bob Fromm left. I want to write about important things.*

Sausalito was beautiful on this sunny day in June. On the previous week, such heavy fog had enfolded the town that it had reduced visibility to a few yards of the surrounding bay. It made her feel they were an island unto themselves. On such days San Francisco was not in sight, nor Angel Island, and certainly not the East Bay. But today was glorious. She rolled down the window of her old VW, and let the morning breeze waft in. Breathing in the sweet air, she said to herself, *This is a good day to be alive.*

Crossing the Golden Gate Bridge toward San Francisco, the sun was already high above the horizon. Not like winter days when she was lucky if it rose before she got to the city. She glanced out toward the ocean. Quite pacified today; no wonder it was called the Pacific. Although, the two years she'd lived in the county of Marin was long enough to know that that body of water had another side— storms of the sea and storms of man, sometimes all in one. She shuddered to remember.

Gwen brought her thoughts back to the moment. She should call Megan Denison— Aunt Megan, as she often called her. Megan Denison had moved into a retirement home, called *The Haven* shortly after her husband Chad died of colon cancer. She had first grieved her son's death, and then her husband's shortly after. Alone, Megan decided that living in a community might help to banish her depression.

In 1967 *The Haven* had no minimum age requirement, and Megan was the youngest ever to enter at fifty-one. So far, this move had worked fairly well. But Gwen knew Megan was not exactly happy, and she felt she owed it to her old friend whom she'd lived with so long, to keep in touch.

As she got closer to work, her thoughts matched her destination. Although generally pleased with her position at *The Chronicle*, her co-worker Dick Jenkins was more than a thorn in her side. Older and with more seniority, he seemed to resent her young vivacious energy. He made snide remarks and twice managed to lose some of her copy. But maybe all that would change if her visit with Mr. Vandermere turned out well.

She found a good parking place on the street and declared, "This is going to be my lucky day."

In the big open room where many writers toiled over their typewriters, Gwen tossed her sweater on her chair, picked up her mug, and noticed Dick wasn't at his desk next to hers.

"If my luck continues," she reflected, "he's taking the day off."

She headed for the lounge. Finding a fresh pot of real coffee, she filled her mug and started back to her desk. Coming around the corner and heading for the lounge, Dick bumped into her, jarring her mug and causing the hot coffee to splash on her white blouse. Gwen felt a burning sensation on her chest, and one of another kind in her head. If he had apologized she didn't hear it as she dashed for the Ladies.

"Maybe this isn't my lucky day after all."

~~~

I don't know why I ever listened to Charlene. She had me under her thumb from the time she told me that she was the oldest. Said she was born four minutes before me. Called me her little brother.

I'm hitching down to Marin County. I left Folsom with fifteen dollars "for a new start in life". I can't believe how high prices have skyrocketed since before I was in the slammer. I splurged today at Oscar's and got a double-

decker hamburger with French fries and salad. But it cost seventy-five cents. I wanted the pie, but that was another thirty-five cents, so I passed.

I should get down to San Rafael by tonight. Last night I slept in a church graveyard. Felt real good being out in the open at night, warm breeze, stars shining up above, and soft grass below. I just rolled around on that grass for a while. It smelled so good, it must have just been cut. It was the first time in thirty-five years that I'd touched real grass. You don't really appreciate things like that until you've been without them for a long time.

I don't get freaked out like some people do, about all the dead folks being there. When we were little Charlene and I used to play hide-and-seek in a cemetery near where we lived in Petaluma. We'd pack a picnic lunch and hike out there. Ma knew, and she said it was alright, but one day the caretaker kicked us out, said it was disrespectful.

I got word a few years back while I was in prison that Ma had died. Mrs. Lewis, a neighbor wrote and told me. I wrote her back, and asked if she was able to find Charlene's address, to let her know. I wonder if Charlene found out. I doubt that the neighbor could find out where she lived.

~~~

Gwen was determined not to let a soiled blouse spoil the talk with Mr. Vandermere, her boss. She did the best she could to wet the dark spot down with paper towels, and then bent down to the electric hand dryer to dry it off.

At exactly ten o'clock she knocked on Mr. Vandermere's door.

He rose and beckoned her in with a smile. He checked his notes and looked up.

"Miss Harris, isn't it? Have a seat. What can I do for you on this beautiful day?"

No small talk here. He looked preoccupied.

Gwen took a deep breath, echoed his smile, and perched herself on the edge of the chair opposite his.

"I'll get to the point, Mr. Vandermere. I understand there's an opening in the news department now that Bob Fromm has left us. I'd like to apply for that position." She sat up straight and looked at him directly in the eye.

"Ah, I see."

She said, "I've brought copies of the work I've done since coming to *The Chronicle*, so you could see— "

He ignored the papers. "What exactly is it you do here, Miss Harris?"

She swallowed. I've covered some society news, also store openings and closings, the films at the park, a Children's Fair and— "

He cut her off.

"You've been here how long?"

"Six months."

He nodded. "Too soon to consider any advancement." He smiled. "You know there's a new hotel going up out there in Marin. I'm sure you can write a fine article on it."

She didn't remember much more of what he said. The bottom line was no, she was not going to get that job. He didn't feel she was ready for it.

As she was leaving he shook her hand and said, "Keep up the good work, and someday— " he cocked his head in an optimistic way.

~~~

I'm getting near San Rafael and now I'm getting nervous. I'm not exactly scared, but it's getting closer to the time when I have to take some action. And when you've loved someone, it's a hard step to take. Of course, all that love turned to bitterness and hate while I was in Folsom. For a long time I felt sure she'd come to see me, straighten the whole thing out. But she never came, never even wrote a letter.

Charlene was always the boss. She came up with good ideas, though, and we had a lot of fun. She was pretty. Folks always commented on her curly blond hair. I didn't mind her being so bossy, though, cuz I never had the imagination she had, and never came up with the crazy things we did. I should have known it would get me in trouble someday.

In prison I spent hours lying on my bunk just planning it out in every which way— how I'd do it. I didn't have a gun, and just the thought of one drives me crazy. Anyway, a gun would make too much noise. But before I do anything, I want her to know it's me doing it, and why. I need her to suffer for what she did, before I kill her. I think she'll know why— that accounts for her hiding and changing her name, and it being so hard to track down. If it hadn't been for this nice librarian at Folsom, who did a lot of research for me, I might never have found out where she is.

When Dad died in a boating accident and Mom became an alcoholic, parental control was a bygone thing. We were so close, me and Charlene. Bold and daring, we were called the Dickens Devils, and were proud of the name. Pranks, like when we went around to neighborhood porches at the crack of dawn with a syringe, injecting vinegar into the caps of glass milk bottles, which caused the milk to curdle. We knew curdling would happen, because Mom used to make sour milk this way for her favorite chocolate cake recipe. I 'd gotten the syringe at Doctor Henson's, after he gave me a shot for something. He laid it on a little table and when he left the room for a minute to get me some medicine, I took it.

Once when we were hitchhiking to San Francisco, we were picked up by a preacher, of all people, who cautioned us on the dangers of hitch-hiking. Even jumping on the back of the milk train when we were kids, just for the heck of it. And the movies—

"I'm going to buy one ticket, Sonny, and I'll go in legit. Then you climb up the fire escape and I'll open the door in the balcony and let you in."

After about three times like this, I said, "Why can't I go in legit, and you climb up the fire escape?"

"It doesn't work that way. What would that look like— a girl climbing a fire escape— people looking up her skirt?"

She always got her way. I started looking back on the shady things we'd done, and how she'd always put me in the hot seat, making me take the greatest risk.

From stealing candy bars in the drugstore, we advanced to stealing beer from the grocery store. Just walked out the door with a six back in our gym bags, right past the cashier. It gave us a high before the first bottle was open. God, those were the good times. Never got caught, not for anything.

Then came the great graduation glory— climbing up the tall radio tower on graduation night and drinking beer at the top, and all the time bellowing out Al Jolson's popular song, 'You're a Dangerous Girl'— except Charlene sang "I'm a dangerous girl'. We were spirited alright.

CHAPTER 2

Gwen was not one to spend a lot of time sulking. She reminded herself that she'd made herself known to Mr. Vandermere. OK, she'd wait, continue doing the best she could with the pieces she was assigned to write.

She called on Megan that evening. *The Haven* was about eight miles north of Sausalito, and then west a bit. She drove there after dinner, so she wouldn't interrupt mealtime. Megan was reading *Gone with the Wind.*

"Haven't you read that before?"

"No, I never did. I've seen the movie a couple of times, though. I'm so glad you've come. I've something to tell you about, Gwen. I don't know what it is, but the noises coming from next door are intolerable."

"What kind of noises?"

"Moaning and groaning."

"Is your neighbor sick?"

"No, she's out and about during the day, happy as a lark. But at night— " She rolled her eyes.

"Does she have a boyfriend?"

"Well, there's a man who comes around. Young enough to be her son."

"Is he?"

"No, I don't think so. And there's these whacking sounds, too. Sounds like she's being hit. I've thought of calling somebody up here to check on her, but . . . well, I like her, and I wouldn't want to embarrass her. She always seems fine the next morning. What do you think it is, Gwen?"

Gwen had a very good idea what it was, and was surprised that Megan couldn't figure it out.

"Sex," she said simply.

"Sex!" Megan seemed dumbfounded. "You mean that kind?"

Gwen nodded. "What's her name?"

"Charlene Osmund."

"Have you spoken to her about it?"

"Heavens no. What do you think, Gwen?"

"Have you talked to anyone else about it?"

"No."

"From what you've told me, that she's fine the next day, I wouldn't interfere."

"Well, I can't stand the noise. I want to change apartments."

"Why don't you turn up your music— drown her out?"

Megan just grimaced. "Will you talk to Mark about it, Gwen? See if I can change? You know him. He likes you."

Gwen sighed. "I'll see what I can do."

She and Mark had known each other through a computer class they'd both taken the year before. Computers were just coming into use in businesses; Mark and Gwen had helped each other work on some of the assignments in class.

Since Megan had decided to go to *The Haven*, Gwen had encountered Mark on two different occasions, once while helping Megan through the interview process required for admission, and recently at a *The Haven* open house, where they'd renewed their acquaintance. He was a friendly, open man who genuinely had the interests of the residents at heart. And Gwen was hoping to get to know him better. Tall and fair haired, with blue eyes, his smile always conveyed a compassionate interest in the person he was speaking with.

~~~

I've spent most of that fifteen dollars on food since I got out. I couldn't believe how prices had gone up. I had to pay twenty-two cents for a loaf of bread and twenty-five for half a pound of bologna. I bought some other stuff that would last me a couple of days. When I passed a gas station, I couldn't believe it— gas had gone up to thirty-three cents a gallon! Well, I've been away for a long time, that's for sure. I got a jackknife just in case that cost ninety-nine cents. I only have a few dollars left. But I've got more important things on my mind today.

If I'm lucky, I'll make it to San Rafael today. The closer I get, the more nervous I am. I wonder what my sister looks like after all these years. We're more than twice as old as on that fatal night. Twenty-six then, fifty-four now. I know I don't look anything like I did then. I'm already losing some of my hair, and what's left is turning gray. I've got a lot of lines in my face. I think all that time in prison made me look older than I am. Wonder if she'll recognize me. Or if I'll recognize her. Of course, she had our money, and probably made a lot more. She's lived an entirely different way than I did, so she's probably better preserved.

We'd been on I-80, so far, 'til this couple I'd been riding with dropped me off. I spied a phone booth there where I called this Haven place, and got directions on how to get there.

Gee, the town sure has grown. Used to be nothing all the way down Highway 16 until you got to town, except a couple of old barns. Now there's houses, a church, an auto shop and everything.

One thing I found out when I was in prison was that my sister was no longer going by the name of Dickens. That librarian, who really knew how to work the vital statistics people, found out that she was going by Osmund. I'd never have found her without the librarian's help.

Anyway, I was on my way with my thumb out again, out on Highway 101. Some guy in a 1939 pickup truck stopped for me. I think there was something wrong with his suspension, and a few other things. It looked like it was held together with Scotch tape and thumbtacks. But I was just grateful for the ride.

Some drivers like to talk, that's why they pick up strangers. Keeps them from being so lonely. This one was a talker. He had to speak up, though, cuz the old jalopy had a lot of rattles.

As soon as I got in, he reached out to shake my hand, and said, "My name's Calvin. What's yours?"

I just said "Sonny," without thinking.

He said, "Where you going, Sonny?"

"To see my sister."

"Good man. Family's important."

I choked on that.

He started talking about his family, then, how there were eight kids, and he was the oldest. He remembered real fondly how they used to play with old rusty hoops from broken down wooden barrels, run races with them. And kick-the-can. His two sisters liked to play jump rope a lot.

"Once I teased them, saying that rope was used to hang somebody on that tree in back. The girls ran off crying. Father whipped me for saying that. Then he set me down and said, 'You know we don't have money for nice toys like some of your schoolmates do. That rope's about all your sisters got to play with. They don't even have a doll, did you ever notice?' I hadn't. He made me feel real ashamed. I apologized to the girls, and made them a couple of cornhusk dolls to play with."

Calvin said he had to play father half the time cuz his pa was working two jobs. He even had to deliver his baby sister. "Nobody else to do it," he said matter of fact.

"How old were you?"

"Reckon I was twelve, then."

"Wow, how did you know what to do?"

"It wasn't that hard. I'd already delivered a couple of lambs."

"We had chickens. They delivered all by themselves."

We both laughed at that.

"Now it's your turn," he smiled. "You got brothers and sisters?"

"Just the one," I mumbled.

"What did you do when you was kids?"

Well, I wasn't delivering babies, that's for sure.

He made childhood sound so nostalgic, I couldn't help remembering the good times with Charlene. I told him about the games we used to play, how Dad got us this football one summer, and how Charlene was as good a player as any of the boys. And the bicycle we shared, riding at breakneck speed, with one of us on the back— usually me.

"You had a great bringing up," Calvin said.

I coughed on that, and went on. "When the iceman delivered blocks of ice, as soon as he was out of sight behind the house, we'd scramble up on the wagon and pick up the little slivers of ice."

"We did that, too," he said, getting quite excited. "Wonderful on a hot day."

This guy was so friendly, I kind of got into it— talking, you know. It felt good to think about something pleasant.

"You know," I said, "Ice-cream was a rare treat reserved for special occasions which required a drive in our old Model T to Knudson's. Then as we sat in the back seat licking our cones, my father, looking through the rear-view mirror, was constantly calling out, 'It's going to drip! Turn your cone, Sonny,' or 'Catch that drip, Charlene.' In later years, we laughed, wondering why we weren't eating our ice-cream outside."

Calvin laughed too, and even pounded on the steering wheel in appreciation.

"No ice-cream trucks in those days cruising the neighborhoods," he said.

"Yeah, I said. But I'd been out of it so long I still didn't know about cruising ice-cream trucks.

He was driving real slow, with every car passing us on the road. Guess he had to with that old rattletrap. I was impatient; I don't know why, couldn't do anything 'til after dark, anyway. And there was lots to see out the window. First, it was country side and cows. Then as we drove south, a lot of buildings sprung up, from car dealerships to motels. I know they weren't there when I was a kid. The road was wider now too, with two lanes going each way.

"Where you coming from?" he asked suddenly.

I was prepared for this. I'd thought it up while I was still in the tank. "I was working at a gated community north of here." Well, it was true.

"Good work," he said.

"Yeah."

I figured I get out on 101, but he insisted on turning west to take me where I was going. I didn't want anyone identifying me later, so I let him pass the place, and about a quarter mile beyond, I said this was my stop.

He shook my hand again and said, "Real nice riding with you, Sonny. You're good company. Have a nice visit with your sister, God bless her."

"Yes, sir," I said, and waved him goodbye.

For a while, he put me out of mind of what I was set to do. He made me get all sentimental. Hell, I had to shake off that feeling. I was on a mission, I couldn't go soft now.

I walked back to the building that was where my sister was living. For a couple of minutes I just stood there on the road looking at it. The place was about four stories high, modern-looking and painted baby-shit yellow.

By now it was about eight o'clock. But in the summer it stays light out until nine. There was a pretty big open space on the west side of the building, with long grasses, *and a little knoll. I sat down behind the knoll and waited. And all that time I couldn't get that driver out of my mind. He was so nice, I was getting mad at him. Maybe that sounds crazy. But I've got a job to do, and I don't want any second thoughts about it.*

When it got dark I approached the building. I had to case the place and come up with a plan. No sense going through the front entrance. There might be someone on duty there. There were some side doors, but they were all locked, not surprising. Then I had an idea. I went around to where there was an underground garage. It had a locked gate, but I saw a car exit. The next chance I had, I'd enter when a car left.

CHAPTER 3

Saturday morning, and Gwen was looking forward to sleeping in. But at seven-thirty Megan called her.

"I haven't had a chance to ask Mark," Gwen started.

"No, no. It's not that. We've had a fire!"

"Where? Was anyone hurt?"

"I don't know for sure. But the first floor is still full of smoke."

"When did this happen?"

"Last night."

"I'm coming over."

When she arrived, Gwen could still smell the smoke. She opened the windows in Megan's apartment.

"It was awful, Gwen. We had to walk down the stairway. We couldn't use the elevator. And most of us were in our nightgowns. We had to go outside, and we couldn't go back in for nearly an hour."

"Did everyone get out alright?"

"Ruth wasn't with us at all. We looked all over for her. Then we realized her boyfriend, Victor, wasn't there either. Turned out they were out together. "

"Where was the fire and how did it start?"

"It started in the auditorium, and there are rumors that someone deliberately set it."

"Arson?"

"Yes. I thought this would be a safe haven, but I'm beginning to wonder."

When she left Megan, Gwen stopped in to see Mark.

He invited her to sit down, and offered her some coffee that she gratefully accepted.

"My first cup of the day. You look worn out, Mark. Were you up all night?"

"Pretty much. Don't understand how that fire got started."

"There's a rumor that it was arson."

"It looks that way. But who would do such a thing?"

"Do you think it was one of the residents?"

"That's actually a possibility. We have a couple of folks who are, how shall I say— "

"Short of a few spark plugs?" Gwen finished.

Mark nodded. "Then again, we have no reason to believe they're pyromaniacs."

"I suppose the police are working on this."

"And the fire department investigation team."

"Was there a lot of damage?"

"No, not too much. The night watchman smelled it, found it and reported it. The sad thing is we had to evacuate the building in the middle of the night, and the poor residents had to use the stairs to get out."

"I know. Megan was upset about that. Speaking of her, she isn't happy in her apartment, Mark."

"What's the problem?" He picked up his pipe. "Do you mind if I smoke?"

She laughed. "What's a little more smoke?"

He offered to put it down.

"No, it's fine."

While Mark tamped the tobacco down in his pipe, Gwen explained her aunt's dilemma.

"Noises, next door."

"What kind of noises?"

Gwen smiled, hoping that would suffice.

"You don't mean— "

"Yes. I guess it's pretty loud. Moans, yelps and whacks."

"Whacks?" He couldn't contain a smile.

"That's what she says. She'd like to move. Is that possible?"

"I'm sorry, Gwen. The only way I was able to get her in was due to a cancellation."

"Well, she'll just have to get used to it, I guess."

"Tell her to turn up her radio."

"I did."

~~~

The next morning Gwen called Mark.

"What's the news on the fire? Was it arson?"

"The investigative team thinks so. It started in a waste-basket in the auditorium."

"Who would do that?" The same question they'd asked the night before.

"In any case, security measures have been put in place. Visitors entering the building have to sign in now at the front desk."

"That's good."

"We're keeping the auditorium locked now. Only staff with keys can open it for events, exercise groups and such. And with this new sign-in system, we'll have a better handle on who's coming and going."

"How are the residents dealing with this?"

"They're nervous, jumpy. I had to get them all together in the auditorium and explain about the new sign-in system, and why."

~~~

Last night the place cleared out real good. Smartest thing I ever did— starting that little fire. I knew it wouldn't amount to much, but it was enough to set off the alarm and get everybody out the building. That gave me a chance to check the place out, get the layout, find where the exits were, that sort of thing.

I thought I'd found a good place to hide until I figure out where Charlene's room is. I was up in the projection booth above the auditorium. At night I could go downstairs to the auditorium, open the door to the outside and take a leak. I never let it shut behind me. But during the day it was more dangerous. And then today came, and it's blistering hot. Besides, they had a program in here with slides on Yosemite, so I had company. The guy that showed the slides was only three feet from me and I couldn't move.

I nearly passed out in the heat behind boxes of old film. Damn, it's hotter up here than it was yesterday. The thought of keeping this as a hideout is out of the question. But where to go? The projectionist was sure taking his time fussing with the projector and collecting his slides. Just when it seemed safe to come out, the guy came back and picked up his soda. Jesus!

I can't wait to get to Charlene. I'll have no regrets there. This is my personal crusade, and the deed is long overdue. Charlene knew how to ruin your life. Charlene knew how to rob you of your self-esteem and personal power. God, she was manipulative. A she-devil, that's Charlene.

I have to get out of this projection booth. Water, that's the first order of business, and then food. Not so much as a candy bar in two days. Oh, and how good a shower would feel!

I'm going down the stairs to the auditorium. Just as I get there I hear voices, people coming in. The only thing I can do is leave the auditorium by the side door. And that puts me right back outside again. Oh, mother!

I'm going to look for a car, an old dirty one, that the owner doesn't even use anymore. Yeah, I could spend the night in it. A dusty one would be best— one that hadn't been driven in some time. Most likely, half these folks never take their cars out at all. The place has a bus that probably takes them everywhere they want to go.

I found just the right car— an old Chevy. It wasn't even locked.

I was lying down in the back seat so I wouldn't be seen, hour after hour. Loneliness and depression set in.

If I was in prison at least I'd be busy. We'd be eating, working or sleeping. We all had jobs. After being on laundry for a few years, I was allowed to take this mechanics class, and then I got to work on cars that belonged to the state, or at least the prison. I liked that job the best. Fixing things always gave me a feeling of pride and satisfaction. Once I even got to work on the car that belonged to the head of the prison.

Anyway, now there was nothing to occupy me like that. I had too much time to think. Why had it all gone so badly? Charlene and me had been good together; she'd been my best friend, ever since childhood. The games we used to play, the lemonade stand in the summer. Who could jump the highest and farthest. Hell, she taught me to read.

~~~

On Saturday, Gwen visited Megan, making sure she was alright, and then stopped in to see Mark. Nothing new on the cause of the fire, but Mark felt better about the new sign-in policy.

They hadn't talked long when Mark said, "I hate to run out on you, but I have a meeting."

"That's fine. I just stopped in to see Megan."

He took her hands in his. "I'll make it up to you."

They walked out of the building together. His car was parked right in front, so they parted there.

Make it up to her? What did he mean by that? Well, it sounded like something to look forward to.

She walked back to the parking lot and got in her car.

But the engine wouldn't start. Over and over she tried, re-fusing to admit that the battery had worn down.

This is all I need, she said out loud. Mark was gone; she'd seen him wheel off. Trying to think, she heard a slight tap on her window, and rolled it down.

A middle-aged man was smiling at her.

"Can I help, miss?"

"My battery's dead."

"Do you have any cables?"

Gwen got out and opened the trunk. Good, they were there.

"Just a minute, I'll bring my car over here, and start it up for you."

"You're very kind."

"Not at all."

The man went back to the Chevy, glad the woman couldn't see how he hotwired it. He drove it over to the woman's car, popped the hood of the car, and asked her to do the same to hers.

He told her to remain in her seat while he attached the cables, and when he gave her the signal, she should start the car. It worked like a charm.

He disconnected the cables and gave them back to her.

They stood outside her car, as Gwen put the cables back in the trunk.

"Thank you, thank you so much. How much do I owe you?"

"Nothing. Aren't we here to help each other in this world?"

"She smiled and turned to leave.

"There is one thing."

"Yes?"

"You should keep your car running for a while so the battery won't die, and I need to get some lunch. I don't know the area, and I'm not sure where to go. What do you say?"

He looked harmless enough. She did owe him.

"Alright. How about McDonalds? You can follow me."

"After you."

When they got there, he said, "What's your name?"

"Gwen."

"Mine's Sonny. Glad to meet you."

Gwen insisted on paying for her own lunch and offered to pay for his in return for his kindness.

The newly established restaurant was the latest hot spot in Marin. They sat at a clean white table on orange seats.

Twice, while they were there, Sonny removed and cleaned his glasses. Was this a nervous habit, or he really couldn't get them clean?

He asked her if she worked at *The Haven*.

"No. I have an aunt in residence, I often visit her. How about you?"

On the way over, he'd thought of an answer.

"I'm interviewing for a job."

"What kind of work do you do?"

"Car mechanics, carpentry— all kinds of things."

It was partly true. He'd learned some skills in those thirty-five years.

"Well then, you have a good chance of getting a job. Where have you worked before?"

"At a gated community up near Sacramento."

She nodded.

They chatted a while until Gwen said she had to be getting on.

He walked her to her car, and as she was ready to drive off, he said, "See you. See you again sometime."

She thought he looked sad.

~~~

Barbara Kelly snapped her suitcase shut, for the last time. She looked around her apartment with satisfaction. She liked living on the first floor. The railed balcony was barely above ground. Due to the steep slope of the land, other balconies on the first floor were much higher off the ground.

No bother with elevators to go up and down for every meal; the dining room was on the same floor, and the trash chute was right outside her door.

Everything was done, and she was ready for the vacation of a lifetime. It would be her first trip outside of the country, a journey to Ireland, the land of her ancestors. Goodness, she'd barely been away from *The Haven* since she'd first moved in ten years ago.

Now she was ready to catch the ten o'clock bed, as she put it, and sleep tight until her alarm went off at six in the morning. That is, if she could sleep, with the excitement she was feeling. In the morning, she would get dressed, lock up her apartment, and be off.

She would call a taxi in the morning which would take her to the bus, which went as far as Sausalito. Then she'd catch another taxi which would take her to the San Francisco Airport.

She had difficulty sleeping, dosing fitfully until three o'clock. Lying awake, she went over all the details of her trip. Yes, she'd packed her passport, airline ticket, itinerary and the pamphlets and books she'd studied for over a year. She was sure she had everything. The anticipation of joining her tour group in Galway filled her with joy. Her father always said that anticipation was ninety percent of joy.

At four in the morning, since she still couldn't sleep she decided she might as well get up. In late June, dawn was already showing its gray face. She pushed into her slippers, remembered that she should dispose of the trash. Pulling the plastic bag from the wastebasket, she tightened its closing and took it out to the hall.

In the middle of the night I walked around the building. Most of the first floor apartments were quite a ways off the ground, but because of the hill, there was one with access to the ground, so I climbed up on the balcony and found the door unlocked. One thing I'd learned the hard way from my sister was to wear gloves; no fingerprints. I stepped inside and closed the door. I didn't see anyone, so I walked through the apartment and on out into the hall.

Against the far wall, she pulled the door open to the trash disposal chute, and made her deposit.

One more thing to do. She'd have to lock the door to her balcony. Just as she turned, she found herself staring at someone coming toward her. What made her sense she was in danger? She opened her mouth to scream.

I can't believe I did that. I keep thinking maybe I'm imagining it. But no, it really happened. I break out in a sweat every time I remember. I try not to think about it. I got so scared, she was ready to scream, so I hit her and she passed out. I couldn't just leave her there. I didn't know what to do with her. And that trash chute was right there.

CHAPTER 4

It was the most bizarre crime Mark had ever heard of, and it had happened on his turf. A resident shoved down the trash chute and found in the dumpster. He could hardly wrap his mind around it.

"We have to consider that it might have been an insider," Detective Arnold Ravinski said.

"That's impossible," retorted Mark Cranson.

"We can't rule out anything," the detective said, lighting a cigarette. Arnold Ravinski was a chain smoker.

"If she comes to, maybe she can identify the villain," Mark said.

"Don't count on it," said the detective. "She's in a coma, and the doc said not likely to survive. She hit her head on the dumpster when she landed— hard.

The maintenance director, the security guard and Mark checked all the doors and found no evidence of a break-in. If the assailant got in through Barbara's door, the door must have been open. It was found shut, but not locked. Fingerprints were taken in the woman's room, but the only ones found were those of Barbara and the housekeeper who cleaned her room. The apartment was sealed off.

The detective and Mr. Cranson looked at the new guest book. Not a long list, as the regulation was only a couple of days old. Inhaling deeply, the detective thumped the book and said, "This does not tell who the visitor was going to see,"

"No," said Mark Cranson.

"Pity," remarked the detective. "There's no way of checking them out. No phone number, nothing."

Was it Mark's imagination that the detective deliberately blew smoke in his direction. It was bad enough that something so horrific had taken place on his watch, but now it was clear that action was being hampered by his new inadequate security system. And that was his fault.

Again, Ravinski slapped his hand on the sign-in book. "What are we to do with these names? Some of them are illegible."

The barrel-chested officer stared at Mark with beady red eyes and bushy eyebrows.

Mark nodded. He felt like a schoolboy being chastised by the principal.

He assumed some of the authority he didn't feel. "I'll instruct all residents to report any visitors they had last night."

"Include the day before as well. The perp may have come in during the day."

Mark nodded.

"We haven't ruled out the possibility of it being an inside job. We may need to fingerprint the entire staff. I'll send some men over."

Ravinski crumpled an empty pack of Pall Malls, tossed it in the general direction of the waste basket, and left the building.

A total disruption of the staff.

But worst of all for Mark was the attack on poor Barbara Kelly. A hodgepodge of feelings collided— sadness, remorse, anger. The heinous attack and the anxiety would spread among the residents. Where to begin?

He'd have to call Paul Henkle, head of corporate. His throat tightened in blatant fear. *The Haven* was one of three retirement homes run by the Bay Area Retirement Homes. Henkle might think it would put a bad name on all the properties. Nevertheless, it had to be done. It would be worse if his boss found out through the newspapers.

He picked up the phone, cleared his throat, and set the phone back on the receiver. After a few deep breaths he picked it up again and dialed.

Paul Henkle was in a meeting.

"Ask him to call me at his first opportunity. It's important."

Mark paced the floor. Then he remembered he'd told the detective that he would ask the residents to inform him of any visitors the day and evening before.

He started a memo announcing the assault on Barbara Kelly. He sighed, composed the memo, asking everyone to report any visitor, stranger or anything unusual they'd seen or heard on the preceding day or evening.

He was tired, numbed by the event. He put his head in his hands.

No. A memo wouldn't do. He needed to talk to them, in person.

The P.A. system, installed only for emergencies like fire, had never been used until this week, and this was the second time.

He tested the microphone, cleared his throat, and began. He didn't want to arouse panic. He'd keep it simple.

"Attention all residents. Please come to the auditorium immediately for an important announcement. Do not rush. Do not overcrowd the elevators. Do not go down the stairs alone."

The auditorium filled quickly. A frantic buzzing swept through the hall, in dread of what awful news would fall upon them.

When it appeared that all residents were present, Mark Cranson walked to the front of the room, and a hush fell over the assembled.

"I have very disturbing news to impart. One of our residents was attacked last night."

More buzzing. Mark waited.

"Barbara Kelly has been seriously injured. She is in critical condition." He was not going to give out specific details.

Another buzz— this time louder.

"In an effort to establish the person responsible for this heinous act, I'm asking you to report any visitors you entertained yesterday or last evening. This way we can rule out known parties. Agnes is at the back of the room, and she will take the names. In addition, please tell her if you saw or heard anything strange. Although it's doubtful that this is a random attack, I urge caution. The attacker could be an outsider." He paused. "Or one of us."

A cry of alarm went up.

"Don't go anywhere in the building alone until this matter is settled. That is all."

Hands shot up as people wanted more answers, but Mark walked out of the auditorium, as the din of anxious voices continued.

He continued down the hall to his office. At least here it was still quiet. He gazed out at the golden hills in the distant west. Somehow, they always comforted him. To the east lay the rest of the town of San Rafael, but it was to the sloping hills to the west, for the most part void of any sign of civilization, that gave him peace.

He'd never dealt with a situation like this. People died, of course. That was difficult. But attempted murder on his patch was beyond his comprehension. He'd been hired because he had a degree in business administration and four years of experience working at St. Francis hospital in San Francisco. Nothing had prepared him for anything like this. He was now supposed to help find the perpetrator, calm the residents, and keep the reputation of *The Haven* from being tarnished. Big shoes were called for, and his were feeling very small.

~~~

I was so cold, I decided I had to get out of the car and move around. It must have been about three in the morning. The moon was ducking in and out of the clouds, looking real eerie sometimes, like Halloween. There wasn't a soul in sight. I jumped up and down and even did some pushups just to create some body heat.

Then a car pulled in, his headlights pointing right at me. God, what a bummer. I got back in the car as casually as I could, and the other car parked a ways away from me. He got out and headed toward the building. He had me real scared, but guess it was a false alarm.

I wanted to get back in the building, but I knew they'd have discovered that woman in the dumpster, and they would be on guard, have extra surveillance, that sort of thing. I had to lie low for a while.

~~~

Gwen drove home from the city, feeling sticky and hot.

She took a shower, and turned on the television news. Within fifteen minutes her phone rang.

"It's Megan. Something terrible has happened."

"Again?"

"You won't believe this."

Adrenalin kicked in, and Gwen was immediately alert.

"Tell me."

"One of our residents was found in the dumpster."

"What!"

"I don't think you can accidentally fall down the trash chute, so she must have been pushed."

"What? Start over." This was not easy to comprehend.

"Barbara Kelly, a resident here, was found in the dumpster."

"Oh, my God! Is she dead?"

"I don't know. We haven't heard anything officially yet. Word of mouth. But I would imagine so, wouldn't you?"

"It doesn't sound good."

"It's so awful, Gwen. Barbara Kelly was a quiet little woman. Who'd want to hurt her?"

There was a pause. Then Gwen said, "Do you want me to come over?"

"No, Dear. There's really nothing you can do."

~~~

Quiet whispers were heard in the dining room. The staff was nervous too. Twice, the clatter of dropped plates was heard, violating the hush, and raising tension further

That day after work when Gwen entered *The Haven*, she went to see Mark first.

"Come in, Gwen. I'm glad to see you. Sit down. Has your aunt told you what happened here?"

"It's awful— poor woman, is she dead?"

"By some miracle she's still alive, but she's hanging on by a thread."

"What are her chances?"

Mark shrugged. "She's at the hospital in a coma, and suffering from broken bones, cuts and internal injuries."

"When was she discovered?"

"In the afternoon."

"I know you have all the rooms checked. Was hers missed in the morning?"

"That's interesting. Nobody checked on her when her knobin wasn't out because she'd signed out for two weeks, so there was no suspicion there.

"If the residents of *The Haven* haven't opened their door and removed the crocheted knob cover by nine-thirty, the person on front-desk duty tries to arouse them by phone. If that doesn't produce a response, health service is called to come up and check on the resident."

"What did finally arouse suspicion?"

"Fortunately, it was trash pickup day, and housekeeping unlocked the fence, and brought the dumpster out of the cage."

"And there she was."

"And there she was, unconscious."

"Lucky that she wasn't buried under a lot of debris," Gwen said.

"If she survives."

"I'm so sorry."

"Because the nature of the crime is so bizarre and unsavory I didn't want to give the details to the residents. But word has gotten out— spread like wild fire."

"Yes. How did the person behind this manage . . ."

"It appears he knocked her out first. She has a huge bump on her head and she's in a coma."

Gwen closed her eyes.

"How do you know she got to the dumpster via the chute?"

"Because the dumpster isn't accessible any other way. It's locked in a wire fenced in area, for sanitary reasons. If she'd fallen from any farther up than the first floor, she definitely would be dead."

"Why Barbara Kelly?"

~~~

Fear struck the residents of *The Haven*. Many were terrified. Active residents who'd been using the stairs to keep fit took the elevators, waiting for others to board the conveyance together. And those on each floor agreed when to meet by their elevator to descend at mealtimes.

The women on the fourth floor had always stayed together in their own group, and knew each other quite well.

"How could it be one of us?" Paula asked.

"That's not certain yet," said Megan.

"Do they mean the staff or one of the— " asked Gertrude.

"Any and all of us are suspects," Peggy Sue supplied. She was very nearly deaf, and always spoke too loudly.

"I never bothered to lock my door before. Now I will," Megan said.

"I'm going to have an extra lock put on my door. And another on my balcony," Gertrude said.

"I'm going to too, as soon as I get my new dentures," Arlene added.

Poor Arlene, with beginning stages of dementia and hearing problems, seldom tracked the conversation.

"Nobody could reach your balcony on the fourth floor, Gertrude," said Peggy Sue.

"I'm not taking any chances. I live on the first floor too," Paula said with her slow southern drawl.

"Where's Ruth?" asked Marjorie.

"Probably out with Victor."

"That makes three times this week." Peggy Sue said.

They returned to the subject of who might be guilty. Suspicion fell on many.

"Well that night security guard has the strength. I put my money on him."

"Who else had access?" Gertrude added.

"What do you think, Megan?"

Megan Denison shook her head. "I have no idea. I'm not a detective." She'd had quite enough of that when her son was murdered in Sausalito, and dear Gwen almost met the same fate.

"The girls on the second floor think it could have been Howard Philips. Have you noticed how he looks at us? Sneaky, he is, with his shifty eyes."

"He patted Jessica on the bottom while they were in the buffet line."

"No!"

"I saw him. They were at the salad bar, near the cucumbers— "

"He doesn't have the strength," Peggy Sue said. "He has Parkinson's Disease."

"I had it too, but it only lasted a week," Arlene said.

A nervous laughter died quickly.

"Did you know that Jessica put an ad in the personals in the paper?" Alice said.

"No. What for?"

Alice leaned closer to the others and whispered. "She said she was looking for a man in the California area who could drive."

"You're kidding."

"I'm not. And get this— she said 'bonus for white shoes and matching belt!'"

This caused a cascading squeal among all of them.

"She didn't. Really?"

"I saw the ad," Alice declared.

"When?"

"Last week."

"Do you still have it?"

"No, it was in the paper in the library. I couldn't take it."

CHAPTER 5

God, I'm miserable. I didn't come to kill that woman! What am I going to do now? Maybe she's not dead. I sure hope not. But if she lives, she could identify me. I can't think about that now. I have to focus, yes focus. I think I'm OK, for now, anyway. I gotta find Charlene's room. I'll see if I can get a hold of that woman Gwen, maybe even get her to tell me where Char's room is. Gosh, I wish I could fall asleep. But I have to have a plan.

~~~

On Friday night when she got home, Gwen was ready to collapse. After working at *The Chronicle* all day, and putting up with Dick's sneers, she was ready to vegetate, have a cool glass of something, and watch TV.

The phone rang.

"Have you had dinner yet?" It was Mark.

"No, too tired to cook."

"May I take you out to eat? I thought we could take a break from the trials of *The Haven*."

Maybe she wasn't so tired after all. "I'd like that."

He took her an Italian restaurant which had aspiring opera singers entertaining the guests on weekend nights. "This is superb. I've never been here."

The handsome tenor sang *O Sole Mio'* and two other songs before taking a break. Gwen was immediately transported into another world, far from the plight of those at *The Haven*. A violinist strolled among the patrons, pausing to serenade at different tables. As he arrived at theirs, playing *Che Cos'e L'amore,* they stopped talking and listened. Gwen felt the sonorous tones of the instrument soothe her body and mind. So romantic, so delicious. She could feel Mark's eyes on her and for a few moments allowed hers to connect with his. She was definitely feeling some vibes.

When the music stopped they checked the menu and ordered ravioli stuffed with mushrooms.

"How is your aunt holding up?" Mark said.

"As well as expected," she said, "given the circumstances."

Mark nodded. "Unfortunately, not everyone is. Many folks are as nervous as a cat on a hot tin roof. Rumors are spreading, fear is growing."

"I know. Maybe I could help you, Mark."

"How?"

"I haven't really thought it through, but it appears these residents need someone to talk to, hear their concerns. You don't have time to do all that."

"But you have a job, Gwen."

"It would have to be a couple of evenings, and maybe Saturday."

Mark looked thoroughly impressed. "It's a great offer. Of course, I could use your help. It sounds like a wonderful idea. Look, don't make any hasty decisions. Think it over, carefully. Be sure you want to do this."

Gwen nodded.

"It will be stressful, I can promise you that."

"I think I can handle it."

When they reached her house, he parked and walked her up the steps. "Good-night, Gwen. Thank you for your company. And about your offer. It's very generous, but really, think it over."

"I will."

That night Gwen couldn't get to sleep. A silent dialogue went on in her head, presenting the pros and cons of her offer to help. She was glad Mark had said to think it over.

What am I getting myself into!

It sounds challenging— I like that.

But you wouldn't have any free time.

To do what? The telephone isn't exactly ringing off the hook.

Well if it ever does you won't be available.

So, I should hold my breath. You're not a real detective, and you're certainly not a social worker, for God's sake.

I know that. But I can talk to people. And it would be a good excuse for hanging around, picking up clues that might solve this case. I want to make Megan safe.

She fell into a fitful sleep, tossing and turning until she could no longer stay in bed.

After doing some stretches, she rustled up some eggs, bacon and toast. A large glass of orange juice and a cup of coffee completed her breakfast. Still early, she put on a jacket on this cool morning, and strode down by the water, listening to the waves, comforting in their predictability. It wasn't long before the lemony sun rose in the sky, something she seldom had time to watch. It was invigorating, and at the same time made her feel peaceful inside.

Sitting on the edge of the boardwalk in front of Sally Stanford's sleeping restaurant she began breathing deeply, focusing on nothing but the regular waves brushing the shore. She began to meditate, envisioning how she'd feel if she followed through on her impulsive offer. After several minutes she imagined how she'd feel if she turned it down. Although there were trepidations about accepting the job, she definitely felt better when she imagined accepting the work. Yes, it was a good opportunity to spend more time with her aunt, and help, if she could, to solve this heinous crime.

Late afternoon the next day when she arrived at *The Haven*, she went directly to Mark's office.

"And the answer is?" he said.

"Yes. On certain conditions."

"And they are?"

"That I don't do anything to interfere with police work."

"Agreed."

"I want to talk to Megan before I meet with other residents."

"Of course."

"I'll go see her now, and come back, OK?"

"Fine."

She rode the elevator to the fourth floor, and escorted Megan and some others to the dining room on the first floor. She had an opportunity before they left her aunt's room to suggest they eat at a table for two, so she could tell her the news.

"I hope you won't object to this, but Mark has asked me to speak with small groups of residents, asking what their questions were, smoothing feathers."

"Gwen, are you sure you want to get involved in another investigation?"

"I'll be careful."

"It's too dangerous."

"I'm only going to be talking to the residents."

Megan shook her head. She knew it was folly to stop Gwen from any pursuit she was on.

"Part-time, of course. I'm not quitting my job at *The Chronicle*."

"I'm glad to hear that."

When they finished their talk, Gwen excused herself to go back to Mark.

"You're sure you want to do this?" he said.

She met his eyes with hers. "Yes. Definitely."

"OK. I'll help in any way you need me. I had some supper sent over. Do you mind sharing it with me here?"

She saw he'd laid a small side table for two with salad and meatloaf.

"Great idea."

While eating, they talked about how she'd go about this, and she agreed to meet the residents on the fourth floor the following evening.

All this time she felt him looking at her in a way that was familiar— the way a man looks at you when he'd like to know you romantically.

The business part of the meeting was over.

Suddenly, Mark put his hand over hers.

"Tell me more about you — maybe your childhood."

"Oh. You don't know about that?"

"No." He looked curious.

Gwen pushed her fork around in the lettuce. She didn't really want to get into it, especially now, when they were trying to de-stress.

She smiled, "Why don't you tell me about your childhood? We'll save mine for another time."

"OK. I grew up in the mid-west— Indiana. Played basketball in high school. Was a 'B' student. Is that enough?"

"No," she laughed. "Connect the dots and fill in the blanks, please."

When they'd finished eating she knew more about him than she did most people. He was very open, admitting to weaknesses and mistakes.

As they were leaving he said, "Promise you'll tell me about you next time."

Since his car was right in front of the building, he drove Gwen back to hers at *The Haven* parking lot, turned the ignition off and leaned over to kiss her. She didn't resist, and what started as a light peck turned into a feeling that aroused her more than she expected. The little peck turned into a fifteen minute overture.

Finally, she pulled away. "Enough for tonight."

He squeezed her hand, got out, walked around the car and opened the door for her.

He waited until she'd started up her engine and was safely moving, before he put his car in motion.

She drove off with her mind in a whirl. Wow. Fireworks. Did she want to get involved with this man— her boss, part-time boss, anyway? She'd be starting off on two adventures now. Was this one any less fraught with trouble than the first?

~~~

Her heart was still in a sweet spot as she drove to work the next morning. Everything she saw took on an intense beauty, as though she'd never noticed it before.

She wasn't even thinking of Dick as she drove into the parking lot.

As she reached her desk, the first thing she heard was, "How did it go last night with the chief, the head honcho of that place? What do they call it? Last Resort?"

A chill ran up her spine. Had he been there? How did he know?

"You looked pretty cozy in that Chrysler of his. Downright intimate."

Jesus, he'd been spying on them in the parking lot! What else did he know?

The only way she could keep a lid on her emotions was to get out of here. She grabbed her purse and went to the ladies' room.

She sat in a stall and felt the tears coming. Running down her face like raindrops on a windowpane, she used toilet paper to mop them up. Could Dick be the— ? No, that's impossible. He doesn't know anyone at *The Haven*. He was just putting her on. But he obviously was there Saturday night to witness her making out in the car. She was glad Mark had waited to drive off until she was moving. If he hadn't, who knows what would have happened?

When she calmed down a bit she had another thought. The fact that he was in the parking lot doesn't mean he was inside the building. For a few moments that gave her some relief. It doesn't mean he wasn't inside, either. But why? And how did he know that Mark was the head 'honcho'? What connection did he have to Mark, if any?

None of it made sense. Her visit to *The Haven* that evening was disappointing because Mark wasn't there. She didn't stay long. After a short visit with Megan, she headed for home. As she came up the steps Denise was coming down.

"Want to join me for a walk? It's a beautiful evening."

"Sure. If you can wait for me to change clothes."

They walked barefoot along the beach, at first in silence, letting the wet sand squish between their toes. The coolness of the water on her feet calmed Gwen. She began to feel in tune with nature, breathing in rhythm with the lazy waves that caressed their feet.

Gwen decided she would confide in Denise. After spilling her story about the wretched Dick, she said, "Does any of this make sense to you? The guy's a real— "
"Dick."

"Oh, Denise," Gwen laughed.

The descending sun glowed on Denise's brown skin. "I think you've got him all wrong."

"How so?"

"The guy's a mental case; I'll give you that. But can't you see it? He's jealous of you— he knows you'll get promoted and he won't— "

"Wait a minute! Are you a psychic or something? I don't know that I'll get promoted."

"Of course, you do. You're bright, a quick study. Oh, and he's got the hots for you."

"Denise, stop!"

Her roommate just nodded.

Gwen sighed. "Well, what am I supposed to do?"

"Stay away from him."

"Easier said than done."

As they sloshed through the gentle waves Gwen was tempted to tell her about the budding romance with Mark. Better wait. Might be bad luck to talk about it too soon.

~~~

Mark had agreed to introduce Gwen to the group on the fourth floor as an employee.

The women— for there happened to be no men on this floor— gathered in their floor lounge the next evening. Mark accompanied Gwen to the room.

"I am pleased to announce the addition of Gwen Harris to our staff. She is here to help answer your questions and listen to your concerns. I hope you will show her the same respect you have shown me."

One or two claps were heard, but most were attentive to what would come next. Mark left the room in Gwen's charge.

Gwen presented a pleasant smile, attempting to radiate some ease and peace among those gathered. The nervous women looked to her for answers. Suddenly she panicked, wondering what in the world she had to say. Well, she'd just have to wing it.

She began, "As the authorities continue to seek out the criminal— "

A cacophony of fearful shouts interrupted her.

"Haven't they caught him yet?"

"What are the police doing about it?"

"Are we to live in terror while they do nothing?"

Gwen tried to calm them as best she could. This was entirely new territory for her. She explained that she was here to listen, and to take their questions to Mr. Cranson, but no, they hadn't found a suspect yet.

She ended by reassuring them that she'd be back to talk to them again.

Seeing the light in Mark's office, she knocked and went in.

Mark rose from his desk and crossed to her. "How did it go? You look shaken," he said, taking her hand.

"There are angry people here," she said. "I don't think I did anything to calm their fears."

"Tell me."

She told them some of the things they'd said, and how she had no satisfactory reply. "The best I can do now is give them an opportunity to vent their feelings."

"Well, that's a tremendous help."

~~~

I'm hiding out in the second- floor laundry room. No-body does laundry in the middle of the night, do they? Anyway, it's warm in here.

When Prohibition came along, Ma was going crazy without her booze. There were folks making bathtub gin down the road, and she found out soon enough about them. She sent Char and me down to get some. It tasted terrible, but for Ma, it was better than nothing. Not long after she was running low on money. Dad had left her some, but it wasn't going to last forever. She got the idea that we could make our own.

By then Charlene and me were thirteen. We didn't have a recipe, but Charlene came up with a plan. She said she heard there was some real good hooch at Smithy's, and if we promised to give him a percentage of what we made in return for the recipe, we'd have it made. Somehow, she got Smithy to agree to it, after they spent about an hour in the back shed talking it over.

Smithy told her you never would have good booze made in the bathtub, so he gave her a list of everything we'd need to make a still. He said the basic ingredients from everything from beer to whiskey were water, sugar and yeast. Yeast is very important. Then you need some coil and a couple of buckets. I forget the rest of the stuff. You can use potato mash to get started.

We got all the paraphernalia from the hardware store and some stuff we had lying around the yard. Somehow, we got it all put together, with me helping Charlene. She was real resourceful that way. She said she needed more information, and didn't need me tagging along.

One night I heard her make some funny noises. I think she thought I was asleep. I sat up and said, "What's that? Are you OK?"

She groaned. "I'm fine."

"What was that noise you were making?"

She didn't answer me at first. Then she said, "Have you ever had a climax?"

"What's that?" I said.

She sighed in exasperation. "It's kind of an explosion inside, sort of like a sneeze, but so much more fun."

"In your nose?"

"No, silly, in your privates."

That didn't make much sense to me. I couldn't imagine enjoying a sneeze in my bottom. It sounded more like a fart to me.

Anyway, finally we got the liquid ingredients together—I guess they came from Smithy's, and made our first batch of hooch. But the whole thing blew up. Ma, Charlene and me cried that day. All that work down the drain.

But the next week Charlene got Smithy to come up to our place, and fix the still. He told her where she'd gone wrong, and how it shouldn't happen again now he'd made it right.

It wasn't but a month or two, with Smithy's help that we got known for having the best moon-shine around. Other 'shiners would come around and want the recipe, but Charlene wouldn't give it to them, wouldn't sell it, either. She was still spending a lot of time at his place, though at *the time I couldn't figure out why. Later I realized how we were paying for his help. He was closer to Ma's age than hers. Not bad looking, I suppose, before he lost a couple of teeth in a fight.*

CHAPTER 6

Gwen arrived at seven o'clock the next evening to meet with the third floor residents. Coming down the hall she ran into Mark.

"I've something to tell you."

"Not now, Mark. I have a meeting."

"It's important."

"Oh, oh, sorry."

They headed back to his office.

Still standing, Mark said, "Missing meals have been reported."

Gwen waited for more.

He took a deep breath. "We have a dumb waiter that takes meals to the health center on the west wing of the fourth floor. The staff up there removes and delivers the trays to the patient. The dumb waiter also goes down to the basement where the staff lunchroom is.

"In addition, when someone is sick, but not sick enough to go to the health center, they can ask for trays to be delivered to their room. In that case, the meals are sent up on the dumb waiter to their floor. Then one of the kitchen employees follows up on the elevator and delivers them to their apartment. If they don't want to be disturbed, they can ask that they are left outside their door. Two residents reported their trays were virtually empty when they went to pick them up, but the kitchen insists they were full when delivered."

"Same meal?"

"No. One last night and one this morning."

"What are you trying to say?"

Mark rubbed his forehead. "I don't know."

"Can you think of anyone who might be taking the food?"

"Well, it could be a resident, I suppose. One meal is included in the basic fee. They can always have more, and it's charged to their bill. I suppose if someone weren't honest, they could steal a sick person's meal, but that would be really— "

"Sick."

"Yeah. And I suppose it's possible that it's one of our employees. Their meals aren't provided."

"What kind of employee?"

"Someone in maintenance or housekeeping, I'm guessing. But that's hard to believe. Most of them have been with us a long time, and we really trust them."

They stood in silence, each running every possible scenario through their minds."

Finally, they couldn't ignore what was on both of their minds. Gwen said, "Are you thinking what I'm thinking?"

"Probably."

"That this interloper is still at large? Stealing the residents' meals?"

"I don't know. I don't want to believe it, but we can't ignore it either."

"No." Gwen felt her heart beating loud and fast. "This is awful news. What shall I do about this meeting? They're expecting me."

"I'll go with you."

"Do we tell them?"

Mark wet his lips. "I think we have to."

"But only the residents on the third floor will be there. Shouldn't they all be told at once?"

"You're right. Let's wait until morning, and I'll get them all down here. Don't want them to go to bed with nightmares."

No, that can wait until tomorrow, Gwen thought. But he was right. Just before bedtime was the worst hour of all to deliver such news. Too bad they had to know. But cautionary measures, which had been relaxed somewhat, had to be reinstated.

"OK, I'll go on to my meeting. Pretend you haven't told me anything."

"Just tell them that since the attacker is still at large they should still exercise all cautions."

Gwen felt somewhat dishonest withholding this new information. Prevaricate, that was a term her Aunt Marie in Michigan had used when she withheld information. It seemed to apply now.

But she couldn't withhold the news. Rumors had spread. The three people who knew about it quickly informed everyone at the meeting, and demanded Gwen address the issue.

She pretended she didn't know anything about it.

"Perhaps the parties got confused and forgot they'd eaten them."

There were murmurs of disbelief.

"Maybe there's a new employee in the kitchen who got confused."

"Most likely it's the same guy who attacked Miss Kelly!" a boisterous voice from the back of the room bellowed.

"Let's not jump to that conclusion," Gwen said as though the idea was preposterous.

"But what if it's true, Gwen?" an elderly gentleman with a goatee asked.

"I suppose it's possible. I'm sure Mr. Cranson is looking into it. Meanwhile, please remember to engage all the security measures we discussed before. Are there any other questions?"

When they rose to leave, Gwen called out, "Please, don't speak of this to others. If there's any truth to it, I'm sure Mr. Cranson will call a meeting for everyone very soon."

She returned to Mark's office. He was still there, inhaling his asthma inhaler.

"They already know," she said.

He nodded. "I was afraid of that. What did you tell them?"

"I felt like a liar— pretended I didn't know."

"I'm sorry to put you through this. Maybe you shouldn't be involved with our problems here."

Gwen was taken aback. "You want me to stay out of this?"

"No, I don't want you to. I just think I'm asking a lot to expect you to handle the residents at this awful time. And I haven't forgotten you have a full-time job."

"You didn't ask anything of me, Mark. My idea."

Why did she feel let down, when she should have felt relieved? He was giving her an out.

He put his arm around her. "Let's go for a drink."

She nodded.

~~~

In the morning Mark investigated the missing tray phenomenon. He talked to the kitchen personnel, found out it were José's job to deliver the meals. José swore that he had delivered them to the residents' doors.

"Did you knock on Mr. Bianco's door?"

"No, sir, he told me he didn't want to be disturbed. I put it on the floor."

"And Mrs. Goldstein?"

"She has a table by her door. Told me to put it on that."

"And were you the one to pick them up later?"

"No, sir. That was Billy."

"Is Billy here?"

"No, he works the afternoon shift. But he tell me the trays at those doors were almost empty when he got to 'em."

"Thank you, José."

The police had been in and out of the building since the day Barbara Kelly had been discovered in the dumpster. Just as Mark hung up the phone Detective Ravinski knocked on his office door.

"Come in."

The Polish detective strode into the room. Before Mark could offer him a seat, Ravinski plopped himself down on the chair opposite the desk.

"I got your call about the missing food. I need you to fill out this form."

The detective pushed two pages of fine print across Mark's desk.

Internally, Mark groaned. Was this the best Ravinski could do with an attempted murder on their hands?

As Mark picked up a pen, the officer bombarded him with oral questions.

"When did this happen?" " More than once?" "The same apartments?"

Mark politely answered the first three questions, and then asked, "Are these the same questions I'm to answer on the form, here?"

Ravinski colored. "More or less."

When the detective left, Mark decided to visit the residents who claimed their meals were missing.

He called on Mrs. Goldstein first. "May I come in?"

"Certainly, Mr. Cranson. Have a seat." The older woman used a cane but otherwise stood erect.

But he didn't want a seat. Elderly people could be absent-minded, forgetful. Perhaps she'd forgotten that she'd taken the food off the tray.

"I sit most of the day," he smiled. "It's good to stand."

He asked her a few questions, the answers to which he'd already heard. He crossed the floor in a manner of pacing, then noticing the tiny kitchen, remarked on how attractive the cupboards were.

"Just had them replaced last fall," she said. "I'm glad you like them."

Nothing here. No tray, empty or full.

"Did you get your breakfast tray?"

"Oh, yes. Blueberry pancakes, my favorite." She stopped and thought. "Oh, but that was yesterday."

"And today?"

"The tray was there, but nothing on it but a little jam, and the silverware. Even the coffee cup was missing. Can you imagine?"

"I'll have another tray sent up for you."

Next, Mark went on to Mr. Bianco's apartment. Nothing there, either.

"I think that guy must still be in the building, Mark."

"What guy?"

"The criminal, of course. Wandering our halls, looking for food. What's he still doing here?"

Good question. On the way down the stairs, Mark was wondering the same thing. The only answer he could come up with was if the guy were still here, he had unfinished business, and what would that be? Oh, God, when would it end?

He called Ravinski. "We need extra surveillance people here."

After some resistance, the detective said, "I'll see what I can do."

Why hadn't he done that before? *The Haven*'s one security guard couldn't be everywhere at once.

~~~

I finally found an empty room. Hallelujah! I heard this leaning lady say to somebody that she'd just finished cleaning the guest room. I got in it real quick.

And bless the Lord, it had a shower. Body odor was bad enough if other people got a whiff of it, but when you couldn't stand your own stink, that was getting pretty bad. There was soap in the tray and even shampoo. Since I still hadn't accomplished my mission, this empty nest was a godsend.

I finished showering, pushed on the little steel knob attached to the glass and opened the door. I toweled off, got back in my clothes and flopped on the bed.

An apartment reserved for residents' guests, so I had to be very cautious. Although vacant now, who knew when occupants would suddenly claim it?

Close watch was called for again. Couldn't hide out in this apartment forever. The quicker Charlene is found and disposed of, the quicker the exit.

Suddenly keys in the lock and voices announced the entry of intruders. Behind the drapes was the best place to hide. That much I'd decided before.

Hoping no one would notice, I made sure no noise or movement ruffled the curtains. Now a couple was inside, talking to each other.

"It's just like a hotel. The bed looks comfy," the man said, plopping down on it.

The woman was in the bathroom. Oh, God. The wet towels!

"Larry, these towels haven't been changed from the last person. Call down and ask for fresh."

The phone did not work— I'd seen to that first thing.

When the couple discovered the problem the man said, "I'll go downstairs and report it."

Damn! That meant the wife would stay in the apartment.

I left the comfort of the temporary pad when the wifey was in the bathroom. Now, where to go? I grabbed a blanket and pillow from this pad, and took the stairs down to the first floor; the utility closet was the only place that looked safe. The middle of the night would be the best time to find another safe spot, but for now, this hole in the wall would have to do.

The linen closet on the first floor was stifling. Finally, I dropped off. At six a.m. I awoke with a start. I had a backache from sleeping slumped against the wall. It was beginning to get light; was it too late to get out unseen?

Out of nowhere, someone was coming down the hall. At this hour! I quick dashed around the corner, but what if this woman followed me in? Waiting, nothing happened. The old lady must have gone back to her room. What had she seen? Anything?

~~~

Saturday morning, a chance to sleep in. But not for long. At eight-thirty the phone rang.

"Hey, kid, want to go for a sail?" Eric asked.

"Sure," Gwen said with hesitation, remembering the time they'd when they'd capsized. Still, on the whole, she knew he was a good sailor.

Eric had been her mother's friend, and he'd been very good to her when she returned to California.

They met at his houseboat in Sausalito the next morning.

After a big bear hug he said, "What do you remember about sailing?"

"Is this a test?"

"Yeah, why not?" he laughed.

Playfully, he asked her to define some of the terms he'd taught her.

"Hey, you get an 'A'. Now, let's see if you can convert theory to practice."

"You mean, do I remember how to sail?"

"Precisely."

It was a beautiful day, and if the wind wasn't quite up to speed, the conversation was. With Eric on the tiller they headed toward Angel Island, as Gwen filled Eric in on what had been happening in her life.

"So that's it— most of my energy has been focused on *The Haven*."

"Because of Megan."

"Mostly."

"You say this guy's still on the loose."

"He could be."

"Gwen, don't do it."

"What do you mean? Don't do what?"

"Get involved with this hunt for him. It's too risky." His eyes were a burning intense black.

"Well, I'm sorry if I made it sound so dangerous— "

"It just is. There's a madman running around. You don't know what he'll do next."

"I'm just listening to the residents, Eric. I'm not creeping into crawl spaces."

"Please. Will you stop, for me, for your mother?"

That was a low blow. "Why are you bringing my mother into this?"

"She wouldn't want you to be in danger, *again*."

Gwen was silent, remembering how her mother had disappeared when she was a child, her whereabouts unknown for years. She'd been sent to live with her Aunt Marie in Michigan. Then after ten years, some bones were discovered in Marin that might be those of her mother. It turned out they were. And Gwen had stayed to discover the cause of her mother's remains being found down a steep ravine on the hazardous road across the mountain to the ocean.

Gwen said nothing. They continued sailing toward Angel Island.

She changed the subject. "Have you seen Denise?"

She had first met Denise when she took a position as a teller at a local bank, and Denise was her mentor. They'd become friends, and when Denise knew Gwen was look-ing for a place to live, she invited her to be her roommate.

"Yeah, I got her to go sailing with me."

"Good, as long as you didn't capsize."

She immediately regretted saying that, but Eric just smiled.

"You know what? I did learn to swim."

"You did! Wow! That's terrific, Eric."

Motioning to the tiller, he said, "Do you want to take over?"

"I'll give it a try."

In the light wind Gwen did quite well. Tacking back and forth across the wind ahead, she had no trouble close haul-ing, keeping as tight to the wind as possible.

"Coming about," she called dutifully every time she moved the tiller over and the bow crossed the wind.

At Angel Island they bought hotdogs and beverages. The hill was beckoning, so they hiked all the way to the top.

"What a view— I can see three hundred sixty degrees."

"It's great," he agreed.

It had been a special day, a great departure from work, and the stress and fear at *The Haven*. But Eric's fear hung like a dark cloud over her head.

She invited him back to the house that evening and made spaghetti and a green salad for him and Denise.

"Anything new on the horizon?" Denise asked, as she speared the avocado in her salad.

"No real clues, no."

"One of the girls said—" she stopped herself and laughed. "Now I'm doing it."

"What?"

"Calling these elderly women *the girls.* That's what Me-gan's group call each other anyway. Don't know if every-one uses that term. But I've heard it often enough."

"The guy's probably left town by now," offered Denise.

"I wouldn't count on it," Eric said. "Denise, try to talk some sense into this girl. She's made herself visible to the residents and no doubt the attacker. What she's doing is very risky." He pushed his plate aside.

"He's overreacting," Gwen said.

"Eric, why are you so upset?" asked Denise.

"Because I couldn't save her mother." He turned to Gwen. "I don't want to lose you, too."

She'd never seen him so emotional. Did he know something she didn't?

~~~

Mark answered the phone.

"Paul Henkle here. How's the investigation going, Mark?" His boss, in the San Francisco office.

"Not much to report, sir. No attacker found yet."

"That detective on it?"

"Yes, sir. He's here most days, poking around."

"And the inmates, how are they holding up?"

"The residents are doing as well as can be expected, sir."

"You know, Cranson, this sort of thing doesn't help our reputation."

"I do know that."

"Good, good. Do what you can to get this thing resolved."

Mark Cranson's asthma was worse than ever. He'd never imagined running a house of horror. The years before had gone smoothly, and the job had suited him perfectly. And now, adding to the stress, there was this pressure from the top.

CHAPTER 7

The next day after work when Gwen entered *The Haven*, the desk clerk told her that her aunt wanted to see her.

"I have a little problem, Gwen. Nothing serious, like the fire."

"Shoot."

"Well, you know I brought my car, and I'm paying extra to put it in the underground garage instead of out on the lot."

"Yes."

"Well, the valet has to bring our cars to us. And one of them is a bit too friendly."

"How do you mean?"

"Well, he goes out of his way to clean my windshield, and I appreciate that, but he seems to have a crush on me."

"Well, enjoy it."

"No, Gwen, I don't. He's started putting his arm around my shoulder. And last week he gave me a little bunch of flowers, from his garden."

"Oh, boy."

"Yes. My question is, what do you think I should do about it?"

"I'd push his arm away, for starters."

"That would hurt his feelings."

"Well, if you're afraid to hurt his feelings, I guess you have to put up with his overtures."

"He must be Italian, you know, he likes to sing. 'O Sole Mio' was his serenade last night."

"Maybe he just likes to sing."

"No, he had me as a captive audience as I waited for the elevator. He was singing to me, Gwen."

"I wish *I* had an Italian tenor to serenade me," Gwen said.

"It's not funny."

"Well, just make sure you're doing nothing to encourage him."

When she left, Gwen wondered if this valet could possibly be the criminal. But what would he want with Megan? Did he plan to use her in some way? The next time Megan planned to use her car, Gwen wanted to be with her.

~~~

On the way to *The Chronicle* Gwen thought about the flower show notices she had to get in by five o'clock, and some other mundane announcements. How trivial it seemed compared to the awful crime at her fingertips. But for now she was assigned and confined to those homey little events that brightened the days of the locals— women, mostly. How she'd love to do the news, at least the local. The real stuff.

That evening, during a fresh fish and salad supper she prepared at home, she and Mark sat opposite each other at the little maple kitchen table.

While they were talking about some of the interesting characters in *The Haven*, she felt his stocking foot touch her ankle. Then as his foot moved farther up her leg, she could no longer ignore the caress. They stopped talking, fastened their eyes on each other. They ate the rest of the meal in a silent dialogue of desire for each other.

Later, sitting on the couch eating fresh peaches with vanilla ice-cream, he cut through her musing. "What made you go into journalism?"

"Guess I always liked to write. In high school I was the editor of our school newspaper. And in college I worked on *The Daily* at the University of Michigan."

"And crime solving— was that an early interest too?"

"No. I never had that in mind."

"You're sure?"

"Come to think of it, in the fourth grade, way before creative writing was in the curriculum, I was writing a mystery, ala Nancy Drew, and the teacher let me read a chapter to the class every Friday afternoon. That was pretty validating."

"And proved you had an interest in crime," he said, playing with her hair.

"Oh, everyone was reading Nancy Drew mysteries then."

He looked at her in a whimsical way. "But it does fascinate you. Tell the truth."

She felt herself blushing. "You know I'm in this because of my Aunt Megan."

"Is that all?"

"Oh, Mark, stop! It's your turn to tell me more about you."

"What do you want to know?"

She smiled and shrugged. Was he married?

"I didn't plan on running a retirement home. But I was a business major, so it fit. I'm thirty-two years old. My wife . . ."

She didn't hear the rest of the sentence. He was married. At least he was honest, albeit a little tardy. Any thought of romance was put to an end. What had she been thinking?

"When I left her— "

"You left her?"

"Yeah." He looked puzzled. "Didn't you hear what I was saying?"

"I guess not," she mumbled.

"And, well I hate to badmouth her, but she could be very volatile. She pushed me out of bed one night, another time kicked me in the balls— oh sorry— and threw a knife at me recently."

Gwen could only listen, stunned.

"I don't pretend to have been the ideal husband, either. Anyway, her target practice with the knife kind of blew the candle out for us."

"That's when you left?"

"Yeah."

They were quiet for a moment. Then Gwen asked, "Do you have your own apartment?"

"I haven't had time to look, with all that's happened at *The Haven*. We split just before the night of the, uh, trash chute incident."

"Staying with friends?" She winced, feeling she was prying too much.

"No. Staying at work. But don't tell anyone. It's just more convenient, right now. I have a rolled-up futon in the closet."

When he left, he held her head between his hands, and slowly kissed her on the lips. Even that was enough to rouse a flutter in her heart.

~~~

On her way to *The Chronicle* on Monday, Gwen was caught in a traffic jam. It was never a zip taking Van Ness Avenue or even Gough, which was somewhat faster. She turned off Gough onto Golden Gate heading for Market. The street was a parking lot. Almost no movement, waiting through three stop lights to move forward at all. What was going on? When she finally reached Market she could see the reason. A parade of young people, all bedecked with flowers and ribbons were coming down the street, with musical instruments, dancing and singing songs. A policeman stood directing traffic. Occasionally, he stopped the parade and allowed cars to pass, but not often enough, as far as drivers were concerned. They started up their own brand of music with the cacophony of horns.

When she finally approached the corner, the officer stopped the traffic just as she reached it and let the parade proceed. At least this gave her a chance to observe what the holdup was. She saw a tangled line of people holding hands, as they snaked through others and back again. A group with a tambourine, flute and accordion tried to stay together as others pushed through. She rolled down her window so she could hear the music. Another group passed by singing *If you're going to San Francisco, be sure to wear some flowers in your hair.* A boy and girl stood necking as others moved around them. Two young women were doing the same.

Where did they get all the flowers? Happy adolescents were throwing them to the pedestrians. A pretty young girl with long green hair approached her car, handed Gwen a flower and blew her a kiss before she moved to the next car.

She had heard of these flower children, but hadn't seen them. More and more of them were immigrating to San Francisco that summer, redefining their values, their lifestyle, rejecting that of their parents. How would it all turn out?

When she finally arrived at work, Dick stood with his arms crossed behind her desk, looking at his watch.

"The boss taking all your energy? Got no energy left for work?"

"There was a parade— stopped all traffic."

"Yeah, the flower children. A bunch of queers and lesbians. Think I'll write a piece about them."

"Would you mind moving, so I can sit down?"

"Sure, princess." He made a bow and moved aside.

It was still awkward moving past him to take her seat. Then he had the gall to stand over her. She could smell his foul breath on her neck.

She took the notes she'd written over the weekend out of her purse. But how was she supposed to compose anything with the ogre leaning over her?

"What's it gonna be today, Doll? Try to write it so I won't fall asleep reading it."

Would he never stop? If she walked away, she'd be admitting he got to her. If she stayed at her desk, the aggravation would continue. What was wrong with this man?

~~~

I'm back in the car. I don't know what I expect to happen, but I'll know it when it comes. I'll get some kind of a sign. In prison, we were always working, eating or sleeping. But now, here alone, with nothing to do but wait, all those memories keep coming back.

Something better happen soon. Maybe I'll find a guardian angel to guide me to my destination. Some might say revenge is wrong, but hey, didn't we fight back in the wars? And don't we have capital punishment in most states? An eye for an eye, and all that. But it's hard to keep focused on my cause, cuz' my mind keeps slipping back to the way it was when we were kids.

I've got to get out of here. Get on with the job.

~~~

"I'd better stay around here this morning," Mark told Gwen on Sunday. Ravinski said he'd come by to go over some things. We're getting nowhere finding the suspect."

"I think I'll go over to the flea Market in Marin City. I need some stuff."

"If you wait 'til this afternoon, I'll go with you. Help you schlep it home for you."

"That would be great. Can you come by around one?"

"I'll be there."

Gwen made a list of what she wanted to look for, including a large frying pan, a reading lamp, and possibly another chair.

When Mark picked her up, she asked how it went with the police.

"They still don't have a clue. They want more information from the victim, and she's still in a coma. According to everyone who knew her, she's a very private person. If she had outside enemies no one knew about it. Only when and if she comes to, can we question her."

Going to the Flea Market was always a delight. People of every stripe were there, calling out their wares, or quietly waiting for the customers to come to them. From used clothing to garden equipment and baby chairs, you could find anything there. Food stands were set up too, so no need to leave due to hunger.

Gwen picked out some kitchen utensils, found a lamp that she liked, and wandered around the grounds with Mark just enjoying the sites— the children running around, and the hotdogs they bought.

She passed another table of mixed kitchen objects. Among them she noted a tray. A sudden thought occurred to her.

"Mark, see this tray? It looks like the ones at *The Haven*."

"Maybe that's where it came from."

"How many of these fit in the dumb waiter?"

"Well, the ones that go up to Health Service are stacked on shelves on a large cart about four feet by five. I don't know. I never counted, but quite a few."

"What are you looking at?" She was staring at something in the distance.

"I thought I saw, oh probably my imagination."

"Who?"

"I don't know. Somebody over by the food section. Looked like the guy who started my car, but now he's gone. I didn't expect to get all this stuff," she laughed. "Good thing I have you along."

"I told you I could be useful."

Mark spied a barbecue grill, and led her to it.

"Wouldn't this be fun? We could fire it up in your back-yard."

"Yes. We had one in Michigan. Have you used one be-fore?"

"No. We'll have to pick up some charcoal. I want to buy it for us. OK?"

"Swell. Let's use it tonight." She squeezed his hand.

She didn't find the chair she wanted, but it could wait.

On the way out of the market, they saw him again.

"Look, there he is!" Gwen said.

Sonny walked by them with a broad smile and nodded 'hello'.

"He's still around," Gwen said.

"Who?"

"The guy who got my car started. He said he was there looking for a job."

They bought some fresh fish and Gwen made a salad and baked potatoes. Mark tried to light the charcoal, but couldn't get it going. Then he realized he needed starter fluid.

"I'm sorry, Sweetie, but I have to go back to the store."

Watching the flames leap up as the inflammable fluid caught fire, Gwen's thoughts suddenly remembered the fire in the auditorium.

"Mark, that fire at *The Haven*, do you think it could have had any connection to what happened to Barbara Kelly?"

"I wish I could say for sure. Could be. There's so much I don't know."

CHAPTER 8

When the housekeeper came to clean her room that day, Charlene asked her to bring up her toy bag from her storage locker in the basement. The girl was always embarrassed at this request, but she complied.

Charlene enjoyed these evenings with the young man who had become a regular in her life. There had been others, former contacts from her rum-running days, but Brutus was the best. That wasn't his real name, but that's what he told her to call him, and she liked it.

She'd met him at a working-class bar in San Rafael, called the Flatiron. After a few comments, he moved over a seat so he could sit next to her. It wasn't so much of what was said that evening, but rather the communication that passed through their eyes. They knew they were a fit.

She'd been seeing him for five months now, and was looking forward to many more. Unrefined, clearly a laborer of some sort, she fancied him more than the contacts she'd made as a bootlegger. His very coarseness, and the rough way he treated her amused and frightened her. But danger had always excited her.

And so was being different. She flaunted it. She bobbed her hair so short, it almost looked like a man's cut. But her manner, if not the way she dressed, was feminine enough. Open and friendly, when the other women got used to her style, they liked her.

Tonight, from a fine collection of stylish and sexy gowns, she chose a low-cut deep purple chiffon which showed off her backside as well as her front. She added a garter belt and black stockings, which, she knew, made the skin above the hose and below the panties tastier than a whole bare leg. Nights like this were the only time she enjoyed wearing feminine clothes, even feather boas and beads.

She didn't know his real name or where he lived, but it all added to the mystery and intrigue of this relationship. Of course, he hadn't given her his phone number either, so she had to rely on him calling her, which was anywhere from twice a week to as long as three weeks, while she waited in frustration for that phone call. He wouldn't ask her if she was free; he'd tell her to be ready for him at a certain time. Seldom did he give her a day's notice. If she had other plans, she'd cancel them. She was always ready.

She chose a fine bottle of Lafite Rothschild Bordeaux from her collection. She knew he'd probably not be able to tell the difference between it and a dollar ninety-five cent bottle of Gallo. But she could, and she meant to please her senses. She decanted it to let it breathe, and sat down to meditate. That's what she called it, but it really was letting her mind go free to imagine the scene she'd create this evening.

The toys she laid out on the dining room table. A flogger, which looked far worse than it felt, a braided long tail which gave a fierce sting, a three layer flapper— more sound than fury, and several other instruments of play.

It was seven o'clock and he was due. A half hour passed. She wanted a drink, but knew he would know and he wouldn't like it. Not alone, she was to wait for him.

When he finally appeared at a quarter to eight her heart started pounding and her breath came in quick short starts.

He hadn't showered, and she could have taken this as an insult, but it was all part of the high she got from playing with someone from a different walk in life.

He smiled at her, took her in his arms, but did not kiss her. He knew she loved the kissing, the open-mouth jaw-breaking type he'd introduced her to, but just as often withheld it. Instead, he pinched her nipple until she pulled back in pain, at which point he pulled her tightly toward him, and made her take more. She knew it wouldn't hurt later when they built up to it, but he'd do it now at the beginning, just to make it hurt more.

He released her, smiled tenderly and took her by the hand to assess the array of toys she'd laid out.

"What have we here? I spy something new, something you haven't shown me before."

He picked up the braided long tail. "This looks dangerous," he said fingering it.

"It is. And it takes practice to use it properly."

He placed it back on the table and picked up a simple cane, swishing it in the air.

"I think I like this. And this and this," he said choosing two other instruments of pleasure/pain. "But first, let's enjoy the wine you've set out for us."

She poured the wine, and they sat on the divan.

"Delicious. Now set it down and say the Pledge of Allegiance."

"What!"

As she recited it, he teased her, nibbling her neck, pinching the inside of her thighs. They couldn't help laughing, as she made many mistakes.

"Now say it again until you get it right."

"How can I while you— "

This time it was going quite well, until he bent her over backwards, so her head was nearly touching the floor.

"And again," he smiled.

The third time he was easier on her and her recitation was flawless.

He led her to the bedroom. "Dance for me," he said.

Charlene signaled that she needed a few moments. Behind her Japanese screen she took off her gown and donned several layers of silk gauze, came back and turned on her record player. The music of *Dance of the Seven Veils* from *Salome* filled the room. Her movements, she knew, aroused him, as she undulating her hips, thrusting them forward, back, turning, exposing her thigh, dropping a veil. The music drove her on into a furious tarantella, dropping one veil after another until she was naked and panting. He beckoned her, pulled her down on his knee, kissed her, then gently pushed her to the floor.

~~~

I met her at a bar. I knew she was a classy lady and didn't belong in this dive. She stood out like a sore thumb. She sat down at the bar— a clear sign she was looking for a pickup— two seats away from me. Before she was even served she looked over and smiled at me. We started chatting, small stuff you know, and then she patted the seat between us and said, "Come on over."

I did, and we talked some more. I can read what women want, even if they're talking French. It's in their eyes. And I knew I was going to bed with this lady before she knew. I had a feeling from the beginning that she liked to play it rough. A little spank and tickle. Or maybe a lot. She was much older than me— probably in her fifties. I've been with a lot of women, but never one of her class. I took on the challenge.

To cut to the chase, after shooting the breeze for half an hour, we were out of there. She took me back to her place, which was some kind of retirement home. Everything about it spelled money, and lots of it. We walked by the front desk, her nodding to the lady there, and up the elevator to the fourth floor. When we got inside her apartment, man, everything in it looked expensive. She poured us a drink, and we sat on her cushy couch sipping. Then she asked me my name. I didn't feel like giving it to her, so I said 'Brutus.' Besides, that was another way to find out if she was the kind I thought she was. She laughed and said, 'I like that.' When she asked 'What do you do?' I said 'Work.' She nodded. By now, she'd caught on that I wasn't gonna get into all that personal stuff.

Without much to talk about, we got down to it. I didn't even kiss her on the couch. I pulled her up to her feet and said, "Let's go."

She led me to her bedroom. I started shedding my duds, and she did the same.

When we got in bed, I kissed her hard, forced her jaw way open. I knew it kind of hurt, but I could tell she liked it. She pulled back and looked at me with wide-open eyes.

"You ever been kissed like that before?" I said.

She shook her head, and leaned forward asking for more.

Well, for an older gal she was pretty good. Experienced, appreciative, and sexy as hell.

I decided the best way to keep her in line, was to not let her get any expectations. I wouldn't set a pattern. She'd have to learn to accept me when I called. And she did. She'd have drinks ready, food too if I told her to. And toys, as she called them, all laid out for me to choose from. And she'd come up with new ones every time.

I didn't tell her much about me, but I had her talk about herself. She had an interesting past— running rum. She was a good story-teller, I'll give her that. She'd make up fantastic scenes for us to act out. I liked that. I'd never met anyone like her. What an imagination. She liked to play slave, and me master. Or I was boss, and she was my secretary. She'd stolen stuff— stapler, stuff like that. I caught her, gave her a choice— fire her, or administer punishment. She chose the latter, of course.

If I could look past a few wrinkles, she was the hottest dame I'd ever known. Sometimes I'd want to see her again the next night, but I always held back. Make her wait. That way, she was more than ready. Once she told me she had a child, but it died of pneumonia when it was four months old. I didn't know whether that was true or not. You never knew with Charlene.

CHAPTER 9

Mark and Gwen went to see *Psycho* one evening when she'd been at *The Haven*. Although Mark had seen it when it first came out, Gwen had not. It created the chills Hitchcock called for, and when they left the theater they were still under the screenwriter's spell.

Gwen found herself glancing down dark allies and holding her breath as they passed suspicious looking characters.

Mark took her hand. "Hey, it was only a movie."

"I know, I'm being silly. I still feel spooked."

When they returned to the parking lot, she thought it had passed, and began to feel the same high she had the last time they were here in his car. Mark moved closer to her on the bench seat, and with very little effort they managed to create a rising of emotions.

Suddenly, with a squeal of breaks, a car tore out of the parking lot.

"Oh, my God! That has to be Dick. He's here again."

"Who?"

"Follow him— quick!"

Stunned and uncomprehending, Mark hesitated.

"Go, please follow him."

He did as directed.

"I have to get his license plate. That's my co-worker, I'm sure."

Mark wheeled around the corner. "What are you talking about?"

"My co-worker, Dick. He was here before. He admitted it. He saw us in the car making out. He even called you the 'head honcho'."

"Why didn't you tell me?" he said as he ran a red light to catch up.

"I don't know. I haven't had a chance. Guess I didn't want to bring the seamier side of my job into our relationship."

"But he could be our assailant."

"I know. I mean— I'm sorry."

As Mark slammed on the brakes to avoid a car pulling out of a driveway, Gwen hit her head against the window.

"I'm sorry. Really sorry. Are you OK?"

"Yes. Just a small bump."

"I think I've lost him. At that last curve— haven't seen him since."

They turned around, looking carefully into driveways where he might have darted.

"No luck."

They drove back to the parking lot.

Mark turned to Gwen. "Let me see your bump." He turned on the dim overhead light.

"It's OK, really."

He pushed her hair off her forehead. "You do have a bump."

"No blood, is there?"

"No, thank heavens."

He kissed the bump, and then he kissed her lips gently.

"I'm going to follow you home," Mark said.

"You don't need to."

"Oh, yes, I do."

"Thank you," she smiled. "I'll accept."

When they got to Sausalito, they both parked their cars, and Mark walked her to her front door.

"Is your roommate home?"

"Yes, the lights are on."

"Good. Then I'll be on my way. Put some ice on that bump."

He kissed her softly and said goodnight.

"Denise?" she called as went in the house. "Denise?"

Gwen walked from room to room. No answer. No Denise.

She locked the door. Finally, she turned out the lights, tucked herself into bed and tried to go to sleep.

About fifteen minutes later, the doorbell rung. Shaken, she sat up in bed.

Oh, my God! Who could it be? Go away!

The doorbell rang again. Too curious to stay where she was, she got up and crept toward the voice. She felt she was back in the film again.

"Who is it?" she called through the door.

"Police."

Police? What could they want with her?

Gwen put the chain on the door, and opened it. She couldn't see the dark figure, and the porch light had been out for months.

"What do you want?"

"May I come in?"

"Why?"

"I have a report of 'hit and run'."

"I don't understand."

"Your neighbor saw you scrape his car, and you didn't leave a note."

"When was this?"

"This evening."

"I don't think I did that. It's midnight, and no time to come calling. Call me tomorrow."

She shut the door, double bolted it and went back to bed, thinking she wasn't even sure he was a policeman. Harder to sleep than ever, she lay awake wondering if she'd made a mistake not letting the officer in. Still, she didn't believe she'd scraped anyone's car, and midnight was an unthinkable time to call on someone for such a matter.

The first thing she did in the morning was to walk a block up Main Street to examine her car. It was old and dirty; there were a few bumps and dents, but she didn't see anything recent. And what part of her car should she be looking at? She supposed if it were true, it had to be on the passenger side. She examined both the front and rear, rubbed a dirty dent that she recognized as being there when she bought the car.

She had a suspicion who had reported her— the man who walked his growling pit bull every night, and had a matching personality. She'd noticed his car in front of the space she'd parked in last night while Mark waited for her across the street. But his car wasn't there now.

~~~

At seven-forty in the morning Mark dialed Gwen's home phone. There was no answer. He was still concerned about her safety, so he called her at *The Chronicle*. She wasn't there either. Well, perhaps she was on her way to work. He'd try her later.

A staff meeting was coming up in five minutes at ten o'clock. He'd try one more time. Someone picked up; again he asked if she'd come in.

"No sir, Miss Harris has not arrived yet."

Fortunately, he didn't have to lead the meeting. It was about changing the laundry services, and the director of that department conducted the meeting. He barely re- membered anything that was said.

He put his head in his hands and tried to breathe. He picked up his inhaler and sucked in its relief. It helped him breathe, but did nothing for his spirits. He had to find out if she was alright.

When he was put through to her department a voice said, "Roger Davis."

"Miss Harris, please."

"I'm sorry she hasn't come in today. Can I take a message?"

"No, no thank you." He hung up.

He tried her home again. No response. Where was she?

~~~

Gwen decided to go to the police station and try to iron
things out. Only a few blocks down Bridgeway, she
walked.

Officer O'Brien sat down in a small cubicle on one side
of a desk; she sat on the other.

After Gwen explained the situation, the officer excused
himself to find the report. She looked around the space.
Not a picture, nothing on the desk. The space was void of
any style or human touch. He came back with it in two
minutes.

"Here it is," he said.

"Then, the man who came to my door really was a policeman?"

"Yes. Officer Schmaltski."

"I had no way of knowing who he really was."

"He must have shown you his ID."

"I couldn't see it." She didn't want to go into detail as to
why she was being paranoid last night.

"Look, when will his shift start? I'd like to talk to him—
clear things up."

"He's gone on vacation for two weeks. He turned it over
to the District Attorney."

Gwen's heart sank. "District— couldn't he have turned it
over to another detective?"

"No. It doesn't work that way."

"What can I do?"

"You'll probably be charged, and given a court date."

Her head was swimming. How could this be happening?

"I advise you to get a lawyer."

The officer's squealing swivel chair gave voice to Gwen's desire to scream. She shuddered. A lawyer? How could this be happening?

Damn, if only I'd let the detective in last night!

~~~

Mark decided to drive to her house. Maybe something had happened. He didn't want to dwell on what that might be. The traffic on 101 was light, and it only took him fifteen minutes to reach her house in Sausalito.

He knocked on the door. No answer. He could peer partially into the living room windows from the porch, but nothing appeared out of order. He couldn't leave it at that. Walking around the house, which was built into a hill, he could see that the back part of the structure was on ground level— no porch needed. He found a cement block, moved it to the window and tried to peer in. The shade was mostly drawn, so the vista was small, and in the shadows. He walked up the hill to where he'd watched her park last night. Her car was still there!

~~~

Gwen left the police station, shocked and bewildered as she walked home. Taped to the front door was a note scrawled in large scribbles.

"Bitch, you didn't leave no note when you hit my car. I'm gonna report you to the police. You'd better hope yer insurance is good."

She tore it off the door, and went inside. If he'd just written the note, then he must be home. She went to look for his car again. There he was, standing beside it with his guard dog.

I'm the one who needs a guard dog.

He recognized her. "Come back to yer scene of crime?"

She presented a brave front. "Show me the damage you think I caused."

He walked to the rear of the car. "Right here. Me and the dog seen you do it."

There were what appeared to be a couple of recent scratches where he pointed.

"I don't recall hearing or feeling anything. There's no new damage to my car."

"And we seen you trying to clean yers off this morning where it got marked up."

Gwen was frightened of this man and his dog. The pit bull picked up on his master's energy and growled at her.

"Look, I don't think I did it, but if you're so sure, I'll pay for the damage." Anything, to get this ogre off her back.

"Damn right you will."

"Cash."

"Cash? No way, gimme yer insurance info."

"I'd rather pay cash. If my insurance is involved, my rates will go up. Get an estimate— "

"No way, girlie, you're tryin' to avoid the law! I'm gonna file another report— you tryin' to scam me that way."

"I'll get a lawyer." She walked away, hoping the man wouldn't sic his dog on her.

"Cunt!" he yelled after her.

She held her breath until she was safely behind her locked door. Then she did some deep breathing. *The Chronicle!* She hadn't even thought about her job since she'd gone to the police station that morning.

Calling the office to apologize for being late, she got a busy signal. She got in her car and raced across the bridge to work.

As she reached *The Chronicle*'s parking lot and was about to get out of her car, another car pulled into the lot. Could it be? Yes, it was Dick, probably coming back from lunch. He didn't see her. She waited until he'd gone in the building to walk over to the car and get his license number. It was a gray Ford. She took a mental picture, wrote down the license plate, and walked into the building.

Dick was at his desk. Gwen sat at hers and tried to focus on the task at hand. How hard it was to think of anything beyond the two big issues facing her — the attempted murder, and her hit and run charge. Now she was supposed to write about the opening of a new park. She began typing, anything, just to let Dick know she was busy, not to show an Achilles heel that he could take advantage of.

A phone call came through to her. It was Mark.

"Are you alright? Where have you been? I've been trying to reach you for hours."

"I'm fine. I can't explain now."

"But— "

"Really. I'll see you after work."

Reluctantly, Mark agreed.

She attacked her new park article again, as hostile eyes bored into her head.

"Don't you have anything to do?" she snarled at Dick.

~~~

Where was Gwen? It was seven p.m. and she hadn't even called. He thought she'd be here by six. He knew she was OK— at least she was a few hours ago. But what was going on with her? Not home nor at work in the morning. Wouldn't talk to him when he finally got a hold of her - And now late.

He lit his pipe and paced the floor.

A half hour later Gwen was at his door.

"Where have you been?" he all but hollered.

"Don't you start in on me."

"I've tried to reach you all day!"

"I had one hell of a day, and I don't need any flack from you!"

"Gwen— "

"I'm not accountable to you!"

He looked hurt. "Well, excuse me for being concerned about you."

"Not like this, no."

"Gwen, please— "

She waved him away. "I can't take any more. It was a mistake to come in the first place."

She left the office. He tried to stop her, but she stalked off.

He sank into the chair at his desk. What had he done? How had everything gotten out of control so fast? He'd never talked to an employee like that. And to have spoken that way to Gwen. . . it made him cringe to think of it. She probably did have one hell of a day, and instead of offering her some TLC, he'd lit into her as if she were at fault. The unsolved attack was getting to him. Worrying about Gwen had driven him nearly frantic.

Should he call her when she got home? Should he go over there? No, better let things cool; he'd call her tomorrow.

CHAPTER 10

I'm still in this old Chevy, trying to plan things out. My mind keeps going back to the past.

About two years after we began making money selling moonshine, Uncle Fred moved in with us, to help out, he said. He helped a little, but mostly he sat and slurped the stuff up. Smithy kept coming over and using our still, which he said was better than his, to experiment. We learned you can make moonshine out of most anything—corn, any kind of grain, and even tree bark. Some of it turned out good, and some of it was terrible. Charlene learned to hold her liquor real good, but I'd throw up if I had more than a couple of drinks.

We were making good money, and Charlene went into town and got herself a whole new wardrobe. I couldn't imagine why, doing the kind of work we did, and never going anywhere.

But it wasn't long before a couple of men started coming around in a brand new car. I knew they had an eye for Charlene, especially the tall one. But after a few weeks Charlene surprised me one night by telling me that these men were bootleggers.

"Then what do they want our hooch for?"

"They say if we go with them, they won't be stopped by the agents. If there's ladies in the car, the agents don't get suspicious. And we'd make some money just riding along. Riding along, that's all we have to do. It will be exciting! What do you say?"

"Sounds awful risky to me."

"What's life without a little risk? We're the Dickens Devils, remember?"

"What about Ma? We can't leave her."

"Sure we can. She's got Fred now."

"Her brother isn't all that reliable, Charlene."

"Brother? You didn't buy that line, did you?" She laughed so hard she said she nearly wet her pants.

I turned real red then and blurted out "What about Smithy? Would you leave him?"

"As quick as this." She snapped her fingers.

I argued some more with her, but she was determined to go whether I came or not.

I didn't want to go, but I wasn't going to let her leave without me.

A week later we packed up and left Ma and Fred to run the business.

"It's a new adventure," she squealed as we climbed on to the red leather seats of their Ford V-8.

"The best part is the part you can't see." Bingo explained how it looked ordinary, as it should for moonshiners, but it had been modified. With great pride he told us how these modifications could conceal storage compartments in roof linings, gas tanks, engine compartments, wheel wells and under floorboards.

"Have you done all that?" Sis asked in amazement.

"No, not yet. But we did get it fixed to hold cargo in the wheel wells and under floor boards. We'll show you."

"Heavens to Betsy", Charlene declared. *"And these leather seats— that's what I love."*

"Well, they're not standard either. Had them converted. Perty, huh?"

As Charlene continued to admire the interior, Bingo went on to explain that as the business grew, as he called it, more revisions would be made. But first, they have to get super stiff suspensions to keep the car from sagging under an additional 1,000 pounds of cargo.

Clive and Bingo were dandies, alright, decked out in the latest fashion with spats and stylish felt hats. Charlene was *always dressed like a fashion model, but I was still in my overalls until we stopped in Santa Rosa, where she helped me pick out some decent clothes. I didn't know whether to feel foolish or divine. I was beginning to get whiskers, so Charlene got me a shaving brush and mug, and some gooey stuff to make my hair behave. She told me I didn't have to look as plain as God made me. I even got some slick black dress shoes to replace my old boots.*

Bingo was the tall one, who made it clear that Charlene was his and his alone. Clive got stuck with me in the backseat. He was kind of shy, and I was too, so for a few days we didn't even talk. Then he started teaching me how to play poker, and that helped to pass the time. He was nervous, too, always afraid when we passed the Federal agents, for fear we'd be caught.

One time we were stopped, and with a stash of the real thing.

Bingo rolled the window down and said, "What can we do for you, officer?"

"Sorry, sir," the officer said. "I didn't see the lady."

"Quite alright," Bingo said with a broad grin.

The agent waved us on. Bingo certainly had a lot of charm.

At night we'd stay in hotels. Not the best, and out of the way, if the men could find such. At first the arrangement was that Charlene and I would sleep in one room, and the men in the other. I was a pretty sound sleeper. However, if I woke up in the night I'd see two heads in Charlene's bed. By morning there was only hers. Soon, that changed, and Clive and I slept in the same room, the romantic couple in the other.

~~~

Mark tried to time his call to Gwen in the morning at home before she'd be leaving for work, but not so early as to wake her up. The phone rang and rang, but no answer. Was she still mad at him, suspect it was him calling and not pick up? Or was there some more sinister meaning?

Just as he hung up and poured his third cup of coffee for the morning, Gwen knocked on his open door.

"May I come in?"

He rose. "Of course. I just tried to phone you."

"I'm sorry about last night."

"No, I am. I didn't mean to light into you."

"I know. And I shouldn't have walked out."

"Please tell me what's going on."

Gwen plopped down in a chair and took a deep breath. "Remember following me home to make sure I was safe?"

"Yes."

Gwen shook her head. "I got busted for hit and run."

"Hit and run? You're kidding."

"Mark, did you hear or see anything?"

"When I followed you home? No. Is that when it happened?"

"I don't think it *happened* at all. But that awful neighbor I told you about with the pit bull accused me of hit and run."

"You mean that night?"

"He called the police. And that's who came knocking at midnight. I was scared to death and wouldn't let him in. He said he was a policeman, but I didn't know if I should believe him."

"What a hell of a time to call, even if he was."

"That's what I thought."

"Then what?"

"In the morning I tried to call him. When he wasn't in, I was so scared I went to the police station. He wasn't there, of course. I talked to another officer who said Schmaltski just started a two-week vacation! He told me that Schmaltski had turned it over to the District Attorney. Can you imagine?"

"No, I can't."

"And that I'd probably be charged,and have to go to court!"

"This is bogus."

"I know, but what am I supposed to do? The officer told me to get a lawyer." She sighed. "It feels like a horrible dream."

Mark put his arm around her.

"I don't know what to do," she said.

He kissed her gently.

"You can't do anything right now."

"And to top it off I had a call from the dentist's office yesterday saying I'd missed my appointment."

He pulled her toward a private corner of the office, and held her closely. "I'm so sorry. Really sorry."

Maybe it was all the pent-up frustration of Gwen's current events, or maybe it was pure desire, but she wanted nothing more than to forget all the problems and just be cocooned in his arms.

"May I see you tonight?"

She nodded.

"Your place?"

With her face in his chest she agreed.

As he walked up the porch Mark could hear Judy Collins singing *Someday Soon*. Gwen had quite an LP collection of Judy Collins, Joan Baez and other popular folk singers. The music inspired him to take Gwen into his arms as soon as he saw her. That now familiar feeling that tornadoed through her body, took over and she was again in a state of bliss.

The front door opened and a very excited Denise burst in.

"Gwen, Gwen, got something to tell you!"

Gwen pulled apart from Mark.

"Guess what? I'm getting married!"

"You're what? You are! When?"

"Very soon." She patted her belly.

"You're not— you are!"

"Yes. And we both want it."

"That's great."

"Who's your friend, here?" Denise asked, glancing in Mark's direction.

"Oh, right. You haven't met. Mark, this is my roommate, Denise Johnson, Denise this is Mark Cranson."

Mark rose to greet her. They chatted for a while, and then Gwen and Mark went out on the porch.

"Gosh, that's a shock. Guess it shouldn't be. She's been seeing Sweet William for some time."

"Sweet William?"

"William. But she's called him that so much, that now I'm doing it."

"She'll be moving out, I suppose."

"I don't know. This was her place when I met her, maybe she'll want me to move. I don't know, we'll work it out."

As he kissed her goodnight he said, "And that hit and run matter— I think it will blow over."

~~~

It was great getting away from this place, and finding that flea market. I didn't expect to see Gwen there, but there she was with some guy. Probably her boyfriend. What I really want is to get her to show me Charlene's room, but I can't figure out how to do it, without her suspecting.

I'm in some sort of costume room now in the basement. It's got wigs, old-fashion dresses. Props, too. Old wagon wheels, palm trees. A good place to hide, I can duck behind anything. We did a Christmas play once at Folsom. I was the second angel from the left.

Reminds me of how when we were with Bingo and Clive one morning, driving through the early fog toward the ocean, Bingo started teasing Clive about when they didn't have any girls to travel with, so Clive had to put on a woman's dress and wig, too— just to fool the agents. Charlene was laughing, and turned around to the back to tease him some more. Poor Clive turned thirteen shades of red and purple, he was that embarrassed.

"It helps," Bingo said," but if they get you out of the car you ain't fooling anybody."

"I didn't do so badly. That agent let us go without a search."

Bingo said, "Yeah, I reckon he had poor eyesight."

Then came the day they told us how we could really help if we had pockets in our coats.

"They'll hold almost a case of hard liquor," Bingo said.

They got me a long coat to replace my jacket. Charlene had to make her own clothes growing up, so she didn't have any trouble sewing those pockets in for us. They looked kind of like the ones for putting shoes in that hang on a rod. They were in a removable lining in our coat, with the bottles on the inside, so they didn't show. Sure made us look fat, and our coats heavy, though.

You never knew what was going to happen next if you were a bootlegger. One night they took us to a speak-easy. I was totally amazed. The guys dressed up, and Charlene said we had to, too. I knew what a speak-easy was, but had never been to one before. The band was playing jazz and ragtime, and you should have seen the dancers. They were wild. A couple of women even got up and danced on a table, and the main singer was sitting on the piano and her bare legs went all the way up. Bingo and Charlene started dancing right away. I never knew Charlene could move like that, but Bingo swung her around him, under him and every which way. Clive and I just watched in amazement. They only came back to the table long enough to catch their breath and have another drink.

We weren't selling moonshine anymore. We'd ride out toward Pt. Reyes where the genuine article came in from Canada. They didn't have prohibition. The cases were usually Scotch, and we'd load them up in the hidden crannies of Bingo's car. Then we'd drive down to Sausalito to the Walhalla Restaurant, situated on the water, where we'd get paid in cash. From there it was put through a trap door to awaiting speedboats tied up to the pilings below the decks. Then it was whisked across the Bay to supply the San Francisco speak-easies.

I was always kind of scared, but Charlene laughed it off, said where was the fun if there wasn't some danger? She really loved it. The men were paying us pretty good, and Charlene liked to shop for new gowns to wear dancing. She had Bingo around her finger, so he'd get her anything she wanted. He even bought her a big diamond ring, just so they'd look married when they checked into a hotel.

CHAPTER 11

It was Saturday morning. The golden hills to the west had always beckoned him. Impulsively, he decided to ask Gwen if she'd accompany him on a drive. She agreed.

"This is delightful," she said as they traveled west. "I haven't had time to go for a drive in months."

"Nor I. I think we both deserve a little R&R."

They drove out Sir Frances Drake Blvd. through small towns sprouting up, then into the gorgeous redwoods of Samuel P. Taylor Park. They were holding hands, except when sharp curves demanded two hands. The trees were so tall and majestic they made a great canopy above, creating a supernatural atmosphere as the sparse sun and shadow danced in the semi-darkness.

"It's mystical," Gwen declared.

Then suddenly, they were out into total sunlight again in farm country. After the small village of Olema, they took the road out through Inverness, past Tamales Bay to the ocean.

Mark said, "I love Marin. I have to make time to enjoy more of it."

"One cannot live by work alone?"

"That's right."

He parked close to the ocean.

"Oh, look at it. I haven't been at the beach in so long."

"Are you hungry?" Mark asked.

Gwen looked surprised.

"I brought a little picnic."

"You did?"

Mark opened the trunk, took out a blanket and a grocery bag.

They walked toward the water, listening to the waves crash against the shore and the gulls shriek as they dove for fish.

Here and there were enormous trees washed up in a storm. Mark placed the blanket in front of one.

"We can use the log for a backrest."

"You think of everything." She smiled up at him, and he brushed the hair out of her face.

They munched on sliced meat sandwiches, apples and potato chips.

"Sorry, I forgot to bring something to drink."

"It's OK. The apples are juicy."

"You never told me much about you. You were born here, then you left, and then you came back. Right?" He said.

"Right."

"You've kind of avoiding telling me what happened."

"It 's not very pleasant. But here it is in a nutshell."

"You don't have to talk about it— not if you don't want to."

"It's OK. When I was ten, my mother disappeared. We were living with Megan's family then in Sausalito. My Aunt Marie in Michigan came and got me, and I lived there until I went to college at the University of Michigan. Then in my last year I was notified that remains of a body had been found which might be my mother's. I was able to get hold of old X-rays which proved they were."

"I'm sorry. I mean sorry about her death."

"I was determined to find out how she died, so I stayed on in California and did some detective work."

"I see."

"And here I am. I never left."

He smiled. "Just the facts ma'am?"

If you want the emotional side, I'll end up in tears."

"OK, never mind. I want you happy."

Just then a gull swept down and snatched half a sandwich off Gwen's plate before either of them could stop it.

"Oh, my God, they're so aggressive!"

"They certainly are. Here, have mine." He offered her his sandwich.

"No, you eat it."

"I'm not hungry."

"I'm not either."

They laughed.

When the food was gone, Mark rolled up his pants. "Let's get our feet wet."

Walking along the wet sand, they jumped back and forth, playing with the waves, but not wanting to get soaked.

Mark bent and picked up a stick. Then he wrote in the wet sand, "I love Gwen."

She looked at in astonishment, stunned. It seemed so early. But it put her in high spirits.

He took her in his arms and kissed her. They walked farther down the shore around a curve, and found a couple curled up together.

"We're not the only ones. Love goes around the world," he said.

"It certainly does."

After a crooked stroll along the water's edge, as they played with the waves and with each other, a breeze blew over them, causing a slight chill.

"Let's go back to the blanket."

They turned around and walked back. When they came to the spot where Mark had put his love in writing, they couldn't find it.

"It was somewhere around here."

"The waves must have washed it away," she said.

Somehow it seemed like an ominous omen to her.

When they reached the blanket, they lay down and curled up in it to keep warm.

"Here," he said pulling more of it over her shoulders. "You'll get cold."

"Now you won't have enough," she laughed, giving it back.

They kissed for a long time, while Mark's hands found her soft breasts, and roamed down her thighs. Finally, as a mother and child strode by, they broke apart to dampen their ardor.

They walked back to the car hand in hand, happy they'd had this time together, away from the troubles of *The Haven*.

Not willing to end the day, they headed back to Gwen's apartment. Picking up pizza and beer on the way, Mark returned to the car.

"I didn't forget something to drink this time," he said.

It was hot in the house, and both were perspiring.

"I have to get you a fan," Mark said.

After their simple supper, desire brought them into each other's arm again, and soon they were in Gwen's bed.

Forgetting the temperature in the room, they created a heat that neither could remember feeling before. Or at least the present moment had blocked out any past such summit.

They were still in foreplay when they heard the front door slam and Denise calling, "Gwen!"

She burst into the bedroom. Taking in the scene before her, she backed out quietly, murmuring, "Sorry, sorry."

Gwen looked at Mark. At first embarrassed, she saw something funny about it, and began to laugh. Mark followed suit, and soon they were burying their heads under the covers to conceal their glee.

There was no continuing the previous activity. They dressed and joined Denise in the living room.

"What's your news, roommate?"

"Listen, I'm really sorry— "

"Forget it."

"Look at this, Gwen."

She'd torn a note off the outside of the door and brought it in.

"What is it?" Gwen demanded.

"Listen to this! 'You are a public nuisance. You go around hitting cars. You will pay for this, Bitch!'"

Mark grabbed the note. "What in the world— "

Gwen told Denise about the so-called hit and run, and how, because she hadn't let the policeman in, the case had escalated to the District Attorney.

"This can't be happening to me."

"Go talk to someone at the court. Maybe they'll drop the case," Denise offered.

"Good idea, and do it soon," said Mark.

They discussed the inciting incident some more.

On the porch when Mark was leaving he gave Gwen a light kiss and held her tightly. "Keep your doors and windows locked."

Gwen said, "Windows? In this heat?"

"Be careful. Be careful of this man."

~~~

Gwen went to her Karate class on Monday night. She'd first taken it to fulfill a physical education requirement at the University of Michigan, and had kept it up ever since. It was good exercise, and it helped to keep her fit. Who knew when she might need it?

When she got home, Denise was pouring over a brides' magazine.

"I had no idea you were getting married. You never said."

"You're never here."

Gwen had to the truth of that remark. "It seems like you only just met William."

"Almost a year."

"Really? How far along is the baby?"

"Four months. You haven't noticed my protrusion?"

"Sorry." She glanced down at her friend. "Well, really, you don't show much."

"Gwen, will you be my Maid of Honor?"

"I'd be honored. When will it be?"

"Three weeks from Saturday."

"That's very soon."

"It will be a small affair at City Hall, and a reception at Sally's after."

Sally Stanford, of brothel fame in San Francisco, had run for the City Council in Sausalito several times. Gwen had helped her during her campaign for council. Sally also ran a fine restaurant on the water, formerly a beer hall called *Walhalla*, which she changed to *Valhalla*.

"Oh, Denise, this is so exciting. I want to help. I'll arrange the party at Sally's. OK? And the flowers. Who are you inviting?"

CHAPTER 12

E arly the next day Gwen wrote down her insurance information and put it on the windshield of the man who'd been tormenting her. Maybe he'd leave her alone now.

Then, after phoning in to tell her boss she'd be late, she headed north to the courthouse, and sought out the District Attorney's office.

"I'd like to speak to the District Attorney," she told a woman through thick glass.

"Which one?"

"Pardon me?"

"There are several. Whom do you wish to see?"

Gwen was stunned. "I don't know."

She explained the situation to the woman behind the glass. "What can I do?"

"You could try writing to the Expeditor."

"And who is that?"

"Varies."

"Excuse me?"

"Just put your case in writing and address it to the Expeditor."

Gwen left, feeling she was in the twilight zone. Nevertheless, after work that night she typed up a letter that stated her case, and mailed it the next morning. She felt she was sending it into the ethers.

~~~

Mark had to talk to Gwen. It couldn't wait any longer. He had to bring her up to date.

He reached her at home that Saturday morning.

"Please come. I need to talk to you."

"What about? I have some errands to do today, Mark."

He said nothing.

"Can't you tell me over the phone?"

"No. I'd come to you, but I don't think I should leave here."

She sighed. "I'll be there about eleven."

Mark looked at his watch. It was ten to eleven. He paced the floor. Gwen would be here soon. He had something to tell her, something he dreaded. Would she still want to help with the case? Would she feel betrayed?

Finally, Gwen arrived, breathless, from running.

"What's up? You found the assailant?"

"No, afraid not."

"You said it was important."

"It is. Sit down, Gwen."

She remained standing.

"Please."

She complied. A strange feeling ran through her belly. She'd been here before, and it wasn't going to be good.

"Would you like some coffee?"

"No, thank you."

"How did it go when you went to see the District Attorney?"

"I couldn't see any of the District Attorneys or make an appointment. Nor could I see an assistant or anyone."

"What did you do?"

"I could only talk to a woman behind a glass window, who I could hardly understand. All she could say was that I should write the expeditor."

"The who?"

"Why did you call me in, Mark?"

Mark cleared his throat a couple of times. He picked up his inhaler and breathed in deeply.

Gwen waited patiently.

Finally, he spoke. "Marlene and I have been meeting a couple of times recently— on her request."

Gwen knew what was coming.

"You want to break up." Her lips were taut.

"I don't *want* to, Gwen. I have to. At least for now."

She waited for him to say more.

"We decided to give it another try, on the condition that she get help."

Silence.

"I'm sorry, about us," he said.

"So am I."

"I don't desire you any less— "

"Please, spare me the details."

Nevertheless, Mark rambled on, trying to soften the news. But Gwen wasn't listening. After a few minutes she rose and quietly left the office. She had planned to visit Megan, but all she could think of now was getting away.

Not allowing the facts in her head to trickle down to her heart yet, she walked resolutely to her car, determined to drive away.

As she reached the parking lot, a familiar figure approached her.

"Hi, Gwen. Remember me?"

She took a good look at him, and pulled her mind into present focus.

"Yes. You're the man who got my car started."

"That's right. How you doing?" His hands were shoved in his pocket.

"Fine."

"I'm fine too."

"What are you doing here?"

"Like I said, I'm trying to get work here. I thought I might speak with another department head today. But guess they're not here on Saturday."

Gwen nodded.

"Wouldn't you say this is a good place to work?"

"I suppose so. Yes, it's very well run, I believe."

She wanted to get away. She wanted to be alone.

"I was wondering," he said and stopped. "I was wondering, you know, I don't know anyone around here. The evenings get lonely. I was wondering if, you know, we could maybe go to a movie together."

The poor guy was sweating, and looked pretty pathetic to Gwen.

"I'm not coming on to you. Heck, I'm old enough to be your father," he giggled awkwardly.

Grandfather, Gwen thought.

"Have you seen *The Graduate?*" he said.

He took his glasses off. Without them, his dark eyes seemed to speak of tenderness and pain. Suddenly, she felt sorry for him. A movie theater was a public place.

Well, why not? Anything to get her mind off Mark.

They agreed to meet down on Fourth in front of Macy's the next evening.

On the way home Gwen felt like kicking herself for agreeing to see him again. Was she that desperate? Or was she too sympathetic for her own good?

~~~

She'd promised to help with the wedding. Only a week to go and she hadn't done a thing except send out invitations to the handful of people Denise wanted to invite. Denise had insisted she send an invitation to Mark, and so she had. Now she regretted it. Surely he wouldn't come now that things were so different.

She'd have to buy a dress suitable for a maid of honor, decide on flowers. What else? It was hard to put her head in that framework with everything else on her mind.

On Saturday morning, Denise said, "Let's go shopping, girlfriend. Get those dresses."

"Good idea. If not now, when?"

They went downtown San Rafael and headed for Macy's on Fourth Street. Without too much trouble Denise found a simple dress she liked, but Gwen didn't see anything that appealed to her. Maybe she was too depressed about the break-up with Mark. She just couldn't get into the wedding game. Denise tried to cheer her up. They sauntered down Fourth Street, and wandered into a small boutique. Denise pulled out three dresses that she liked, showing them to Gwen. Finally, Gwen chose one of them and tried it on.

"It's lovely, Gwen."

It fit, so she bought it.

They stopped for lunch at a pizza dive.

"Look, Gwen, I think this thing Mark's going through with his wife won't last."

"What makes you think so?"

"It wasn't working before. What's changed?"

"I don't know. I'm sorry I'm not good company."

Denise took her hand. "You're just fine."

On the way home, they bought candles and napkins for the reception.

"I'll arrange for the flowers on Monday," Gwen told Denise.

"Then we're all set. Listen, Gwen, if you want to keep the apartment, you can. I'll be moving in with William."

"Oh. OK, if you're sure. I'll need to find a roommate."

"You won't have any trouble. How about someone at work?"

"I'll think about it." But the only one that came to mind was Dick, and he surely wouldn't do.

The next day Gwen decided she had to visit Aunt Megan. She had no intention of seeing Mark.

As she walked toward the elevator, Mark approached her.

"Can we talk?"

"What about?"

"I, I was wondering if you're still interested in helping with the case."

"Maybe."

"Could you stop by, after you see Megan?"

"Afraid not. I have a date."

A swell of victory rose in her throat. That ought to set him on his heels. And she hadn't lied, either. She was going to a film with Sonny.

"Who with?" He couldn't believe he'd said that. It was none of his business.

"If you must know, he's a nice man who came to my rescue in the parking lot a few days ago when my battery died. He's applying for work here."

"Well, have a good time."

She walked away, feeling a smug satisfaction, having let Mark know she was not drowning in sorrow.

Actually, she was. Well, not drowning, but feeling pretty awful about the sudden end to what was beginning to look very promising. She kicked herself for getting so involved with a married man, even if he was separated. Separated was not divorced.

Thank God, she hadn't gone all the way with Mark. *Thank you, Denise for bursting into the room.*

She missed all the things she used to do with her roommate. With her wedding coming up next weekend, she saw little of her old friend.

But she had a new distraction with Sonny. Not the same as being with Mark, not romantic, but at least someone to do things with. There was something mysterious about him, which made her want to know him better. And something vulnerable behind those soft, brown eyes.

~~~

Curiosity drove Mark to ask the department heads which of them had recently interviewed a man for a job. None had.

Mark thought through the implications of this. That meant either Gwen had lied to him, or the man had lied to Gwen. He thought it was the latter. Initially he was just curious about this man; now he was afraid for Gwen. He called her.

"Gwen, it's Mark. I'm sorry to bother you, but there's something you should know."

"Yes, you told me yesterday."

"No, this is something else that involves your safety."

"What?"

"The man you said was looking for employment here?"

"Yes?"

He winced to say it, knowing she'd realize he'd been nosey, but he had to. "None of my department heads has interviewed anyone recently."

Gwen swallowed. What did this mean? Was he the assaulter? Why else would he lie? What was he doing in *The Haven* parking lot in that old car?

"Gwen, are you there?"

"Yes."

"That's what he told you— that he had interviewed someone here?"

"Yes."

"Did he say who?"

"No."

"You said you were seeing him tonight?"

"Yes."

"Please don't go out with him. He's dangerous."

"I don't like it that he lied about why he was there, but that doesn't make him dangerous."

"Even if there's a chance that he is— please, Gwen. I care about you."

She wanted to say something like, yes you demonstrated how much you care, but held her tongue.

"I'll think about it," she said. "Thanks for telling me."

He couldn't get Gwen out of his mind. His wife had initiated the idea of getting back together. Part of him thought they should give it another try, but Gwen being at risk made him realize he was in love with her more than ever.

He was wild with despair. This man certainly posed a threat, but Gwen was an adult, and he couldn't prevent her from seeing him. God, if only he hadn't broken up with her, she'd never be in this fix. He felt she was acting on the rebound.

He reached for his inhaler. Where was it? Of all times to misplace it.

~~~

Gwen tried to think clearly. Should she really be afraid of this man? Why had he told her he'd had an interview? Or had he said he planned to? She wasn't sure. She thought he'd said he'd already had it.

Although she didn't much feel like listening to Mark right now on any subject, she decided to act on the side of caution. She had no way of reaching Sonny by phone to call off the date. Her only recourse was to stand him up. Would he be suspicious about that? Angry, yes. She didn't see that she had a choice.

I'm down on Fourth Ave waiting for Gwen. We decided to meet here, by Macy's and then go to a movie. I'm going to get her to tell me where Charlene's room is tonight. I didn't want to arouse her suspicion by asking too soon. No hurry, don't want to rush things.

But I think tonight would be a good time. She trusts me now— has no reason to question my interest. I told her

Charlene was an old friend and I'd have to drop in and see her some time.

Damn, we agreed to meet at eight o'clock. She's twenty minutes late. I wonder what's keeping her.

~~~

At nine o'clock Mark couldn't stand it any longer. He called Gwen. She answered. He breathed a big sigh of relief. Then another worrisome thought.

"Are you alone?"

"Yes."

"Thank heavens. You decided not to go."

"Yes."

"Does he know where you live?"

"I don't think so."

"What does that mean?"

"Well, I suppose he could have followed me, but I don't think so."

"Is Denise with you?"

"No."

"Gwen, I think you should come up here. I don't like your being alone down there in Sausalito."

"Go there, and do what?"

"I'll find you a guest room."

"Isn't that pretty extreme?"

"No."

She thought about it. Maybe he was right. She'd already angered Sonny by not showing up. If he knew where she lived, he'd be very angry, and maybe yes, dangerous. She really didn't know him at all.

She packed a nightgown, toothpaste and brush and started out.

CHAPTER 13

I waited until nine o'clock before I knew that she wasn't coming. I knew I'd made a mistake telling her that I'd had an interview for a job at The Haven. Looks like she found out I lied. Now I've scared her off.

Well, I'll get her, one way or another. I'm going to pack it in for tonight. I've got no better place to park this piece of junk than back there at that retirement place. Anywhere in town, the police would get on to it. Maybe ask me for the registration, or they might be looking for a stolen car, but I don't think so.

Jeez, I didn't mean to go through that red light. What irony, if I get caught for that. Good, no police around.

I'm not going to park in the same spot as before, in case she comes.

Well, here I am. I'm calling it a night.

Suddenly, lights of another car are bumping across the lot, and headed toward me. I'm ducking until the lights are extinguished and the person gets out.

By God, if that isn't Gwen. What a break! I'm on my way.

~~~

It was ten o'clock, and still no sign of Gwen. Mark called her again. No answer. Maybe she'd had battery problems again on the road. He tried to stay calm. He called the hospital to see if she was a patient, from an accident on the road.

Finally, he got in his car and drove to Sausalito. He pounded on her door. it was locked, nobody home. He walked around the street, looking for her car. Nowhere.

Speeding back to *The Haven*, he looked for any sign of an accident on the way.

Finally he called Ravinsky.

"We're working on it. We're working on it, man."

"I'm not calling about that."

"About what?"

"*The Haven.*"

"What now?"

Mark cleared his throat. "Gwen, you know the lady who's working for me now, as a social worker, calming the fears of—"

"Yeah, what about her?"

"She's missing."

"From *The Haven?*"

"No. She's not at home and not at work—"

"If it's not part of the *Haven* case, I can't—"

"It's important. She's been followed, and I think she's in danger."

"How long's she been missing?"

"Several hours."

"Too early to report a missing person. Look, she's probably out with some guy—"

"No, she isn't." He hated to say it, but he did. "She's my girlfriend, and she was supposed to be here."

"Still, you gotta be realistic, Cranson. She's probably cheatin' on you—happens all the time."

Was this some kind of sick revenge because he'd hired Gwen? Mark hung up.

He tried her phone one more time.

"Hello," it was Denise. She sounded sleepy.

"Have you seen Gwen?"

"No. I got in about midnight. I assumed she was in bed, or with you. I'll check her bedroom."

"Would you?"

Denise left the phone. It seemed forever before she returned.

"I've looked everywhere. She's not here."

"Any sign of—of a struggle, anything amiss?"

"No. Was she supposed to be with you?"

"She was coming to *The Haven*, yes. She never arrived."

"When was that?"

"Between eight and nine o'clock."

"Oh, my God!"

"Would you mind terribly going outside to see if her car's there, please?"

"Sure. Hang on for a few minutes. It could be anywhere on the street."

He hated asking her to go out in the middle of the night alone, but he felt he had no choice.

"I'll hold."

He reached for his inhaler. Empty. He'd forgotten to replace it. He tried to breathe calmly. In and out, in and out. It felt like an hour before Denise returned to the phone.

"No, Mark. I took a flashlight. I didn't see it anywhere."

"Then she did leave your place last night."

"Yes, I would say so. This is terrible," Denise said.

"I really didn't mean to alarm you."

"Well, of course, if she's missing, I should know."

~~~

Gwen had a sense that she was being followed in the parking lot. Just as she was about to turn, she felt a hand clap over her mouth. She jerked to get away, but a vice-like grip held her in place.

Who was this and what did he want?

"Thought you'd get away from me, did you? I know what you're thinking."

It was Sonny; she recognized the voice of the person she couldn't see. She was turned around and tried to push in the opposite direction. He pulled her tight into his chest and kept his hand over her mouth.

"You found out I didn't have that interview right? That's why you didn't show tonight."

She nodded.

"You're going to help me do what I came here to do. You got that?" He tightened his grip.

She nodded. Fear pulsing through every cell in her body, she didn't know what else she could do. She needed time to think. Time to see if she could bring this man to his senses. Maybe he had a dual personality. What had he come to do? Her head was spinning.

"I'm not going to fool around anymore. You might as well know the truth."

She tried to pull away.

He forced her over to the Chevy and pushed her in the back seat. She tried to get out. He jumped in beside her and closed the door.

"Don't try that again, lady. I've got a knife."

~~~

Mark decided to call Megan.

"Have you heard from Gwen?"

"No, I haven't. I wasn't expecting her tonight. Were you?"

"Yes." He didn't want to alarm the woman, but he couldn't lie either.

"Well, if she comes, will you let me know?" Megan asked. "Now you have me worried."

"Certainly."

That last possibility, that she was spending the night with her aunt dissolved, and with it an agonizing pain of fear.

~~~

"I'll take my hand away, if you promise not to scream."

She nodded.

He flicked open his knife. It was only a jackknife, but she knew it could do real damage.

"Insurance. Just in case you change your mind."

She waited to see what he would do.

"You have to understand I've waited thirty-five years for this opportunity. I've got a sister in there who let me take the rap for something she did."

Gwen said nothing. She didn't dare.

"I've got nothing against you. But I have to use you for a hostage." He wiped his brow. "Nothing personal."

It was cold in the car, but Gwen was sweating.

"See, I know she's in there. I just don't know which room."

Gwen felt the chill go up her back.

"I've come to even the score."

She didn't want to believe he meant to kill his sister.

"Charlene Osmund. You know her?"

"No." Gwen knew of her. This was the neighbor Megan complained about.

"You're lying. You work here."

She shook her head. "I work at *The Chronicle*."

As soon as the words were out, she bit her tongue. What an awful thing to have revealed to this assailant. She'd only meant to steer him away from any connection to the residents.

"Why do you come here, then?"

"I have a friend."

"Who?"

What had she gotten herself into? She didn't want to put Megan at risk, nor Mark either.

"Who?"

"I can't say."

"Who?" He held the knife to her throat.

~~~

Hearing a timid knock on the door, Mark opened it.

"Come in, Mrs. Dennison."

The room was filled with smoke, as Mark had been filling his pipe non-stop since he began worrying about Gwen.

"You haven't heard from Gwen?"

"No. Have a seat."

"I'm so worried."

"So am I. Can you tell me where she might have gone? Her old haunts? Anything would be helpful."

"I've been thinking about that. But I'm beginning to believe she's met with foul play."

"Let's not jump to conclusions, Mrs. Dennison."

"You don't need to play soft with me, Mr. Cranson. I've been through this before. I lost a son to foul play. I waited, I worried, and in the end, ..." Her voice trailed off. Then, "It's the same feeling now— exactly, déjà vu, don't they call it? The same thing all over."

Her eyes were dry, but her lips and hands were quivering.

"We can't assume anything. Please tell me where she goes if she's not at home or work. Or here."

"She has some friends down in Sausalito. Boat people."

"House boats?"

"Yes."

"What are their names?"

"One of them is called Eric."

"Does he have a phone?"

"I can't remember. I'm sorry."

"Would anyone else know him?"

Her eyes lit up for the first time. "Denise, her roommate might remember them."

It was the first ray of hope they had.

"I'll call her," he said.

She rose to leave. Mark walked to the door with her.

"If you think of anyone else, ma'am, let me know right away."

"And you do the same."

~~~

"We're going to change cars. We're going to drive off this lot in your car."

"What!"

"You heard me. Give me your keys."

"Why?"

She fumbled in her purse for them, and handed them to Sonny.

He reached across her and opened the door.

"Now get out."

With a tight grip on her arm he marched her to her car. Unlocking the passenger side, he opened the door, and told her to get in. She was too much in shock to think of escaping.

Then he got in the driver's side, started up the car and drove off the lot.

He drove down the road in the opposite direction of anyone coming to *The Haven* from town. No streetlights here. Totally deserted. He turned the ignition off, and pulled out his knife.

Gwen was scared to death, but she knew she had to do something to calm this man down.

"Let's talk," she said.

He jerked away. "What about?"

"We began as friends— "

"You're trying to pull the wool over my eyes."

"No, I just want us both to be safe. OK? Why are you doing this? What do you want with me?"

He stared at her a long time.

"OK. I'll tell you this much. My sister killed somebody and let me take the blame."

"Why are you here?"

"Cuz she's here." He motioned to the building. "I'm gonna get her."

Gwen swallowed. "You didn't say anything about her to the arresting officer?"

"I did, but he thought I was just trying to blame somebody else. And then I didn't say anything at the trial because . . ." His voice trailed off.

Softly she said, "Because?"

"Because of the stupid loyalty I had for her. I thought she'd come forward, own up, you know, but she never did."

If she could just keep him talking— "Where did this happen?"

She wanted to know more, much more, but with the knife raised, he turned toward her. "Why you asking so many questions?"

She tried to still her jagged breath. "Just thought you needed to get it out."

He lowered the knife, and looked at her closely. "You ever been arrested?"

"Yes."

"What for?

"Hit and run."

"You?"

"It was crazy. It wasn't fair."

"Then you have an inkling how I feel."

"Yes."

"Thirty-five years in the slammer. Bet you didn't go to jail."

"No, not yet. But it isn't over."

"Tell me."

He got interested in her story, and forgot about the knife. Then he started talking about himself again.

"When she tossed you the gun, what did she say?"

"'Shoot'. She said 'shoot!'"

"And did you?"

"No!" Sonny pushed her down on the seat, covering her body with his. "No!" he screamed. He pounded the seat beside her. "No, no, no! I did not kill that policeman!"

Gwen could hardly breathe. She'd gone too far, asking that delicate question. This man was clearly unstable, and she'd disturbed his hornet's nest.

"I'm sorry," she got out in jerky syllables.

"You better be." He got off of her, and fumbled for his glasses, which had fallen on the floor.

They sat in silence for a few minutes.

Then she had to say it. "Sonny, I have to pee."

He glared at her.

"Really. I have to go bad."

She could almost hear him thinking.

"You can go behind the car. I won't watch you, except your head in the rear view. If you try anything— "

"I'll be back."

She did have to pee. She'd had to for over an hour. She knew he'd outrun her if she tried to run.

She got out and walked behind the car. Looking around, she could see no one. No help anywhere. She hadn't resorted to this way of relieving herself since they were kids. Behind the bushes. In the fields. Using big leaves to wipe themselves. No big leaves here.

She felt her internal organs relax as she let it go. She gazed at the only building in sight. So close to safety. Mark was at his desk or making phone calls. He must be going nuts wondering where she was. If only she could call him.

"Hurry up, there!"

She pulled up her pants, pushed her skirt down and went back to the car.

"Took you long enough."

"I was holding a lot."

"Now it's my turn. You're staying in the car, and if you try to leave, you'll be very sorry."

He got out, shut the door firmly and walked behind the car. When he returned, he said, "We're going to wait a couple of hours 'til everybody's said their prayers and gone to bed, and then we're going in. You're taking me to Charlene's room. For now, you can rest in the back seat."

He got her in the back. "Just don't try anything funny."

~~~

Mark couldn't sit still. He walked out to the parking lot, and scanned it for her car or a moving figure. Not there. My God, that meant she left home, and something had happened on the way. Going back to the office, he felt sick. Another hour passed.

At midnight, he called her home again. Still, no answer. He felt totally helpless to assist the woman he loved. Maybe she was dead, or wounded and lying on the floor.

He'd go back to her house and break in if he had to.

~~~

Denise called Eric, Gwen's houseboat buddy in Sausalito.

"Have you heard from her?" Denise asked.

"About a month ago."

"Not in the last two days?"

"No. Why?" Eric said.

"She's disappeared."

"What!"

"She was on her way to *The Haven*, but never showed up."

"What can I do?"

"I'm not sure."

"Do the police know?" Eric asked.

"They won't pay any attention to missing persons for seventy-two hours."

"How long has it been?"

"Just a few hours, but— "

"She's not with her boss?"

"No. She told him she'd be right over. That was hours ago."

"Jesus."

Denise said, "Can I come get you? We have to do something."

"Right."

~~~

Gwen lay awake for hours, turning and twisting in her backseat bed. She'd run several escape plans around in her head. Maybe he'd fall asleep and she could run for it. But he never did. She could tell he was awake. Maybe if he marched her into the building, as he said he was going to, she could alert the night person at the front desk, who would get someone to arrest him. Maybe she'd scream, and Sonny would get scared and run. The best she could do was play it by ear.

~~~

CHAPTER 14

*S*itting there, wide awake in the front seat, I didn't dare fall asleep. Gwen would run away. I had to stay awake, stay alert. My mind went back to the time we were doing a drop, and had our coats loaded, because we had to park a block away. A policeman stopped us and wanted to search us. I was scared to death. Charlene just looked him straight in the eye, and dared him to. She laughed and said, "If you touch me, I'll bring suit against you for molestation." The officer walked away, without even frisking me. It was not considered decent for an agent or policeman to search a woman. Some say that allowed as how there were far more women bootleggers than men.

Anyway, we became pretty bold because of that and because there were only fifteen hundred federal agents assigned to enforce prohibition for the whole country. And a few policemen to help out in some towns.

It seemed like the more dangerous it got, the more Charlene enjoyed it. Rather than keeping her head down for a while, she'd really want to whoop it up. She'd drink more and sing at the top of her lungs. I couldn't keep up with her.

Then she got the idea that she was tired of working under the men, and we could make more money and have more fun if went out on our own.

"We're eighteen now. Time we were on our own. We've learned the business."

"We don't have a car," I protested.

"We're going to get one, real soon. I've been saving up, and we have enough to buy a used, but powerful car, with modifications."

"They're expensive."

"I've been talking to somebody. He's going to get us a real deal."

I didn't know whether to believe her or not. Sometimes she took my breath away.

"And it's got a big trunk, which can hold a lot of hooch."

"Charlene, we had protection from the men. They had guns. How are we— "

"I got a gun, Sonny." She showed me a lady-sized pistol.

"Oh, God, Charlene. Where'd you get that?"

"Bingo gave it to me, for protection. It's not a Tommy like he has, but it will do."

We carried on arguing for half the night, but as usual, Charlene won. She was going to do it, with or without me.

Two weeks later, she bought her dream car, and off we sped.

"Did you tell Bingo we were leaving them?"

She just kept singing, "I'm a dangerous girl, and I'm havin' fun."

I knew she hadn't told him. I'd have liked to say good-bye to Clive. I noticed she wasn't wearing her diamond ring.

"I had to pawn it to get enough money for the car."

On the road, Charlene was the height of propriety. She always dressed in a proper homemaker way and wore white gloves. I didn't wear gloves, but she made me wear decent worsted wool pants and a proper button down white shirt and jacket. She even got me to wear a felt hat.

In our hotel rooms, she started to teach me to dance, and after a while I caught on to the Charleston. The next time we had a chance to dance, I was determined to ask someone. I was nervous, but I did it. This young lady,

Marsha, danced with me all evening, and said she'd see me there the next night. And if Charlene hadn't rushed us out of town the next day, I know we'd have danced the next night, and probably the next. It was the first time I'd felt anything like a flutter for someone. But Charlene said, business was business and we couldn't get sentimental about anything or anyone.

~~~

She heard the crunch of an apple.

"Want one?" he said.

Her mouth was so dry. "OK."

He tossed her one. She took a bite of it, and then another. But she could hardly get it down, and it was causing her acid reflex to act up.

"I have to pee again."

"You know the rules."

She was hoping that someone would drive by and she could wave him a distress signal. No such luck.

She got back in the car and Sonny got out to do the same.

Then he opened the back door and said, "It's three A.M. Time to go."

She sat frozen.

"Come on. Get out."

She'd been frightened the whole time she was in the car, but now she was terrified. She'd try psychology, and if that didn't work, well, she wasn't sure.

"Sonny, please get in. Let's talk about how we're going to do this."

"Like what? We're going to go in. You're going to take me to Charlene's room."

"Sonny, we need a plan."

"Like what?"

"Please get in."

He climbed in beside her.

"Are you setting me up?"

"For starters, do we walk side by side, or how?"

"No, I want you slightly in front of me."

"With a knife in my back?"

"Not if you don't pull something funny. Look, I don't want to hurt you. But I will if I have to. You understand?"

She nodded.

"Sonny, do you really plan to kill her?"

"What have I been telling you?"

"You've just finished thirty-five years in prison. Do you want to go back there for the rest of your life?"

"That's none of your business."

"I don't want you to."

He was startled. "Why not?"

"Because I think you're too good for that. Is one moment of revenge worth going back to prison?"

"Gotta do it! I told you!"

Her heart was racing. She swallowed twice.

"Well, you don't need me."

"You're my hostage. And you'll show me the way."

"Please, just let me go."

"Enough."

He pulled her out of the car with such force that she almost fell to the ground.

~~~

Denise drove through town, and into the houseboat community at the north end of Sausalito. Eric was waiting.

"What do you think happened to her, Denise?"

"I don't even want to think about it."

"What are we going to do?"

"I don't know where to start."

"Has she told you anything that could put her in danger?"

"There's this neighbor who's been giving her hell about some scratch on his car."

"Is he a mental case?"

"I really don't know. He's yelled at her, left vile notes and filed a police report. Now it's been turned over to the D.A. She'll have to go to court."

"Anything else?"

"I know she works with someone called Dick, and he's harassed her. He even followed her to *The Haven.*"

Eric stroked his graying beard. "Unless one of them is a real crazy, they don't sound serious enough to kidnap her . . . or worse," he said, mumbling the last.

"Well, we can't just sit here. We have to *do* something," Denise said.

"Do you think she might have just had enough, and gone off to be alone somewhere for a few days?"

"She wouldn't do that without telling me. Besides, Mark said she'd agreed to spend the night at *The Haven*, and she didn't show up."

"Let's go there."

With no plan at all, the only place they could think to go was *The Haven.*

~~~

They walked down the dark road, with no flashlight, no moon. If she were ever to attempt an escape, now was the time. What was the point of learning Karate if she didn't use it in a situation like this? With her heart in her throat Gwen broke away and began running. She knew he'd catch up to her.

When he did, she turned to face him, used a straight leg kick to his head. He went down, and she ran. Cursing, he struggled to his feet, ran after her. Again she turned to face him, and this time as he put his arm on her left shoulder, she placed her right hand on his wrist, bent at the waist, twisted to the right, taking him along with her, until he was on the ground. As he lay face down, she jammed her knee into his shoulder with sufficient force to make him moan.

"I won't do it, Sonny. I can't take you there."

She rose and ran again, as he swore at her.

Now the dark, unlit road was in her favor. Before he could catch up again, she left the road, darting down the ravine on the side. She could see nothing, could only hope. Just then she tripped on a rock and tumbled head first down several feet, falling on her face. Though she tried to control it, she emitted a muffled scream.

The sound, of course, drove Sonny to her location. As she could hear him coming after her, she could only pray.

Terrified, she could hear him stumbling around in the long grass and rocks, looking for her. When he found her, at first he did nothing but look at her, breathing heavily. Then he mumbled, "I ought to put you out of your misery."

But he bent down, and said quietly, "Where does it hurt?"

She looked at him in amazement. "My knee, mostly, and my face."

"Can you walk?"

How to answer.

She could say she couldn't and be left here alone without help. Or she could walk, and end up forced to show him Charlene's apartment.

"I don't know."

He was amazingly strong. He brought her to her feet, and half carried her up the slope.

"Now be a good girl, behave yourself. Any more tricks and you'll meet the same fate my sister's going to."

She knew he was assisting her only to accomplish his own goal. Limping slowly, he helped her along the road back to the residence.

Gwen knew that at this time of night the halls would be empty. They went toward the front door. With luck she could signal to the person on desk duty that she was in trouble.

Sonny said, "Walk softly. Don't make any noise."

Entering the building, the desk was on their left. With her fingers crossed they crept by it. There was no one at the desk! Sonny pushed her toward the stairs. "Safer than the elevator."

"I can't, I can't climb all those stairs."

"Then we'll take the freight elevator. Nobody using it this time of night."

She stalled, but he forced her onward, and around the corner. Her knee was throbbing. She felt she must be living in some kind of violent nightmare; this couldn't really be happening. What was she about to witness? Then what would become of her? If he hoped to get away with his crimes he couldn't afford to let her live. And poor Megan, right next door. What if she awoke and got involved? Too terrifying to think about.

Leaving the lift, they walked down the hall to Room 413. Loud sounds were coming from inside.

Sonny stared at Gwen. "What the hell?" he whispered.

"I guess she has company."

"Jesus!" He hadn't counted on this.

Gwen watched his eyes dart back and forth, racing through his options. Suddenly, he turned her around and marched her back to the freight elevator.

On the way down he said, "Was that noise what I think it was?"

"I understand she has a friend— "

"A lover?" he said in disbelief.

"And he's here at all different times."

"Why didn't you tell me?"

"I didn't think of it. And I'm not informed when he's expected."

"You told me you didn't know her."

"I don't. Only what I've heard."

"Now I have to plan all over. Shit! Back to your car."

As they left the lift he had her by the arm. Perhaps the clerk would be back now.

Sonny said, "Not that way," and propelled her in the opposite direction toward another stairway, leading to the basement.

CHAPTER 15

Gwen!" a voice called from the lobby. Two people came running toward her.

Gwen turned. It was Denise and Eric.

Sonny pulled her, dragged her along. Then he let go. And he was gone.

Her friends caught up with her.

"Where did that guy go?" Eric asked.

Sonny was nowhere in sight. Eric took off in a sprint. He didn't know the building. He ran down the hall, glanced both ways at a cross passage, chose the left. It was a dead end. He retraced his steps, chose the other direction, which ended with stairs leading to the basement. Knowing this was one of many directions the kidnapper could have taken. Still, he ran down as fast as he could, hoping he'd find the door to the outside. If this goon had been in the building all along, surely he knew this escape route.

Denise hugged Gwen, then looked at her face. "You're bleeding! He did that to you?"

Gwen shook her head. "I fell."

"What did he want with you?"

Gwen just shook her head. Now that she was with friends, whatever stamina she'd had evaporated. "I need to sit down."

Mark had heard the noise in the hall and came dashing out. He saw Gwen on the floor and ran to her. "Thank God!"

"Let's get you to a chair," Denise was saying.

Together, Mark and Denise helped her to a nearby bench. It was clear Gwen was in no condition to talk, so they did what they could to comfort her.

Finally, Eric returned. "Lost him."

"Let him go," Gwen said weakly. "He has a knife."

"Stay with her," Mark said. "I'm going to call the police."

He dashed back to his office.

When he returned, Mark said the police were on their way. He and Eric supported Gwen as they stumbled to the office and got her in a comfortable position.

"It's my knee," she said, holding it, and raised her feet up on a chair.

He asked Eric and Denise to stay with her while he accompanied the police through the building. "And do something about her face."

"I was going to," Denise said.

Denise got some water and cleaned Gwen's face. The scratches were mostly superficial, but she had one rather deep cut on her temple. The man at the front desk had returned from a pit stop, and furnished a box of band-aids and some ice for her knee.

It was not Ravinski who came, but three uniformed officers. The one who seemed to be in charge approached Gwen.

"Can you describe the man who kidnapped you, please, Miss Harris?" the officer asked.

"He's medium height, brown eyes, in his fifties, I think." She paused. "That's not very helpful, is it? Oh, and he wears glasses, black rims."

"And his hair color?"

"Mostly grey, starting to bald."

Then the officer— she couldn't remember his name— asked her to give as complete account as she could of the events that had taken place.

She pulled herself together enough to give a fairly articulate report, of how she was grabbed in the parking lot, dragged into his car, later forced into her own car and driven off the property. At this the officer interrupted her.

"Miss Harris, what is the kidnapper after? Did you find out?"

"Yes." She sat up straight. "He's here to kill his sister, Charlene Osmund. She's a resident — "

"Did he?"

"No, he forced me to take him there, but she had company. We didn't go in."

The officer immediately sent one of the other policemen to guard Charlene's door.

Mark returned to his office, anxious to be with Gwen and see how she was doing. He thanked Denise and Eric for being in the right place at the right time. He told them he was going to put Gwen to bed in a vacant guest room, and stay with her.

As he led her up the elevator, Gwen said, "Why am I shaking? I'm not cold."

"You're in shock."

"Mark, does Megan know?"

"Yes. I've called her, told her we have you back, rumpled, but safe."

There were a thousand questions on his mind: How did it happen? Where did it happen? He'd missed most of the detective's questions, and she was too tired to be grilled again. He knew he'd have to wait for the answers until Gwen got some rest. What she needed now was comforting and sleep.

He pulled down the blankets. Too tired to undress, she fell upon the sheet, fully clothed, except for her shoes. Mark stripped to his underwear and climbed in beside her, holding her, just holding her until she fell into a sound and safe sleep.

Although he'd had no more sleep than Gwen, at seven o'clock Mark awoke from habit, took a shower and got dressed. He sat beside her on the bed, watching her. During the night, and even now, from time to time she moved her head from side to side and made disturbing sounds.

Should he wake her? Better not, let her sleep. He called down to the kitchen and had some breakfast sent up for her, and quietly left the room.

At eight o'clock the police were back in the morning, scouring the building and grounds again. This time Ravinski was with them. He wanted to talk to Gwen.

"She's sleeping."

"Time is important if we're going to catch the guy. I don't even have a description."

Why not? Mark thought with irritation. She gave it to the officer last night.

Reluctantly, Mark returned to the guest room and woke Gwen.

"I'm sorry, sweetheart. Ravinski needs to talk to you."

She nodded. He tried to help her to the bathroom.

"I can walk."

They went downstairs together, where the detective was waiting. He seemed kinder, gentler than he had before. Mark sat beside her, soaking up the answers he too, was eager to hear as the detective questioned her.

Ravinski started by asking the same questions she'd been asked the night before. Again, she gave a description of Sonny, told them how she'd been caught as she crossed the parking lot, and forced into his car.

"Then where's your car?" Mark blurted out. "I looked all over for it!"

"He didn't want it found here. He made me give him the keys and we left the grounds, but not far."

"Where were you before that?" Ravinski asked.

"In his car. At least he said it was his."

"What did it look like?"

"It was an older model Chevy. Blue."

"Did you get the plate number?"

She shook her head.

"Under those conditions?" Mark demanded.

"I'll have to ask you to keep silent, or leave the room, Cranson."

"Some sleuth you are," Ravinski mumbled in her direction, but loud enough to be heard.

"I'm not a professional! I never pretended to be, and I'm not perfect!"

It was the most energy she'd put out since she'd gotten back.

Ravinski just stared at her. Then he put in a radio call to his officers on the grounds, telling them to look for both the Chevy and Gwen's car, and to be aware that the suspect might be in one of them.

Lighting a cigarette, Ravinski said, "Miss Harris, what was this Sonny after? What did he want?"

"He wanted me to take him to his sister's apartment."

"Why?"

Gwen swallowed. Slowly, she told them what she knew— that Sonny had taken the hit for something that his sister did, which put him in prison for thirty-five years, and his determination to make her pay.

"Pay?"

"He was going to kill her."

"And what was it he took the rap for?"

"He didn't tell me."

"Who is this person?"

"Charlene Osmund."

Mark said, "She's still alive. An officer's been at her door all night."

Ravinski turned back to Gwen. "What did this man want with you?"

"He said I was his hostage. He said he didn't want to hurt me."

"Did he? Did he cause your bruises?"

"N, no, not directly. But he's very disturbed. I never knew. . . when he might."

"Did he have a weapon?"

"A jackknife."

"Did he threaten you with it?"

"When he got scared, yes."

"When he got scared?"

"Yes. Sir, I think he was as scared as I was. But he's not a hardened criminal."

"Are you defending this man who terrorized you?"

"No. No, I mean you have to understand him— "

"Understand him? Hold his hand? Give him therapy?" Ravinski was on a rant, pacing the floor, lighting up again.

"He needs help."

Ravinski gave a sigh of disbelief.

Gwen knew it was highly probable that Sonny had pushed Barbara Kelly down the chute.

"Is, is Barbara dead?" she asked.

"No. By some stroke of fortune she's still alive. Fell on a lot of rubbish which softened the blow," Mark said.

"Oh, thank God!"

"Not unharmed, however. She's in the hospital recovering from broken bones and internal injuries. She's in a coma."

"May I go now?" Gwen said.

"Just a few more questions, Miss. Knowing what you do about this guy, where do you think he would be now? Where would he go?"

Gwen shook her head. "He's either still in the building, or he took off."

"Could you be more specific?"

"I don't know."

"We need your help, Miss Harris. We need to apprehend this man."

"He may have gone back to that Chevy. That's all I know."

Mark intervened. "Will you release Miss Harris now? She's been through a lot, and needs to rest."

Ravinski looked defeated. "Yeah, she can go, for now."

Mark went with Gwen back upstairs to the guest room. "How are you feeling?"

"Tired, dirty. I need a shower."

In the room, Mark tested the phone to make sure it was working, turned the water on in the shower for her.

"I just want to be alone for a while. Thank you for everything, Mark."

"I was scared to death for you. I'm so glad you're alive and all in one piece."

He held her gently. "Be sure to bolt the door when I leave, and call me if you need anything."

"Let Megan know I'm feeling better. I'll call her later."

"I will."

Gwen took a long, hot shower. She felt nothing she could do would bathe away the stench of what she'd been through. Finally, she pulled back on the little knob on the glass and stepped out of the shower.

Climbing into bed naked, wondering how she had sustained a reasonable composure as long as she had. Now all she wanted was the sleep of oblivion.

~~~

The residents had to be told. As expected, when they knew the assailant was possibly still in the building, they were as chickens in a barnyard when someone approaches. Sneaking down the hall to gather in Gertrude's apartment, they exchanged their thoughts.

"I think I'll go stay with my daughter in Georgia," Paula said.

"If it comes to that, I'll go to a local hotel." Peggy Sue announced. "The safest place to be."

"I've been having nightmares. Last night I dreamed I got arrested," Alice said.

"What for?"

"For ripping the tag off my mattress. It's illegal, you know."

"No, it isn't."

"Then why does it say that?"

They looked at each other. No one had an answer.

"I wasn't sure it was just a dream. This morning I checked to make sure the tag was still on the mattress."

"And was it?"

"Yes, thank the lord. Now that we know that criminal may still be in the building, who knows what kind of nightmare I'll have tonight!"

"You're just a silly goose," Peggy Sue declared.

~~~

The search for Sonny continued. The Chevy remained in the parking lot, unoccupied. Gwen's car was brought back to the lot. Sonny had either taken off on foot, or was still in the building. Or had he found another car to hide in?

Mark insisted that Gwen take a few days off from work, and stay at *The Haven*.

"But this is where Sonny is!"

"He's probably gone, but in any case, I think you'd be safer here than at home, especially since Denise isn't there very much now."

"He isn't gone, Mark. Not for long anyway. His whole objective is to kill Charlene."

Gwen felt she was between a rock and a hard spot.

"Maybe you'd like to stay with your aunt."

"And put her at greater risk? No, thank you."

They pondered over this. Finally, Gwen said, "I know, I could stay with Eric on his houseboat."

Mark frowned.

"It's not like that. He's twice my age, and he's an old friend. Don't look at me like that."

~~~

Eric, only to happy to help his friend out in this crisis, was more than willing to share his accommodations with her.

"You can have the couch or my bed, and I'll take the couch."

"I wouldn't think of putting you out of your bed. I'll take the couch."

A large man, Eric didn't argue.

For three days he fixed meals for her, crept around so as to not disturb her when she was sleeping. Most of the time he was outside working on his various fix-it projects—lawnmowers, bikes, and an old wood-hull sailboat.

One night she woke up screaming. Eric jumped out of bed, came to her side and woke her up.

"Where am I?"

"You were having a bad dream."

She rubbed her face. "Oh, God, will I ever get over it?"

"You were dreaming about . . ."

"Yes."

"Time heals many things."

He made her some cocoa and toast. "Comfort food," he smiled.

On the third day Gwen had supper ready for him.

"I've let you baby me far too long. I think I'm ready to join the living."

"You went through so much; you needed a good long rest."

~~~

Now that I know where Charlene's room is, I can find it on my own. I decided to lie low for a couple of days until people would assume that I'd taken off. I found a barn on the outskirts of San Rafael. Although there's a house not far from it, the barn doesn't appear to be used for anything, except to store some household stuff. No sign of animals or farming around. I've got to find a way to get in that building when I go back. I don't want to go in through that woman's apartment that I used before. Besides, it's probably sealed off or something. It still gives me the shivers to think what I did to that poor old lady. I was just so scared. Maybe it was all that knee jerk reaction from nights during Prohibition when we had to react quickly. I don't know. But I sure am sorry that I killed that woman. But not Charlene— I'm gonna get her if it's the last thing I do.

I can go back in the building when somebody leaves the garage, and I'll walk in. Now it's time to give that sister of mine her final rest.

~~~

Gwen had just spent her third night at Eric's. The morning of the wedding day, she drove to the florist and bought the flowers Denise wanted: stargazers, her favorite— large, white, with a touch of pink and a lovely fragrance. After arranging them at Sally's, she helped Denise get ready.

"You look gorgeous," she told her friend. The pale green silk against her dark skin was stunning.

Then she prepared herself. Not knowing if Mark would show up or not, she was uneasy. But she tried to put her own feelings aside and share Denise's joy.

The ceremony itself at the Marin City Hall went without a hitch or glitch. William had a best man, and Gwen was the maid of honor.

The reception that followed was when Gwen began to feel tense, wondering if Mark would show up. She hardly tasted the delicious appetizers Sally had prepared. Just before it was time to sit down, Mark walked in. Eric, who was standing beside her nudged her. Her heart jumped. Why was she so nervous? She was still seeing him at work. And he'd been very good to her when she finally got free of Sonny. She looked away, but Mark found his way over to her.

"Sorry I'm late," he said.

"I didn't know if you'd come."

"I wasn't sure I should. But I did accept Denise's invitation. How are you feeling, Gwen?" He looked at her with genuine concern.

"I'm fine."

"May I sit with you, or are there place cards?"

"No place cards. I didn't have time to prepare them."

"You did this? It's beautiful, the flowers and decorations."

"Thanks."

"You didn't answer my question."

"Yes, you may."

With toasts to the bride and groom and the general liveliness of the party, Gwen's spirits rose.

As the bride and groom were leaving, and everyone was gathered at the exit around the deck by the water, Denise tossed her bouquet deliberately in Gwen's direction. The toss was a bit too high, and although Gwen reached for it, the flowers went over her head and highballed into the water below.

After Denise and William took off for Lake Tahoe, Gwen stayed to help collect the flowers and what was left of the wedding cake. Mark offered to help take them to her place.

She didn't ask him to stay.

"Are you sure you're OK staying here alone?"

"I'll be fine."

"I don't think it's safe."

"Mark, I need to be alone. I'll lock up."

He wasn't satisfied, but she was certain.

As he was about to leave, he asked, "How is that hit and run case coming?"

"I don't know if the court will pursue it or not. I haven't heard anything more."

"Perhaps more smoke than fire."

When he left, she looked around the apartment. Even though she'd been there alone many times, somehow knowing that Denise no longer lived here made the place seem empty, deserted.

While looking for another vase she came across the nasty notes from her neighbor. In disgust, she ripped them up and threw them away. Although she'd opted for a court-appointed lawyer should her case go to court, she hadn't heard a thing; perhaps Mark was right and it had blown over.

She put the flowers in different rooms, in an effort to make the place look cheerful. It helped a little, but oh, how she would miss Denise.

CHAPTER 16

When the cleaning lady left, Charlene spread the toys out on the table, choosing the ones she liked best, and putting the others back in the bag. No, better to let him choose. She placed them all back on the table. Next to it she placed the poem she'd written for him, stating her desire to serve him in any way she could.

After that she stepped into a warm bath of bubbles, listening to soft music on the radio. She closed her eyes and started imagining what the evening would be like. They had a new game. He wanted her to describe a fantasy, said it excited him. Like Scheherazade, she came up with a new story every time.

Sometimes, they'd act it out— he playing the master in the south, and she his slave. Or the humble wife of a husband in the 1700s, whose duty it was, according to the preacher, to discipline his wife for all her misdemeanors. She herself, was to keep a record of those trespasses, and he would administer the appropriate punishment at the end of the week.

Charlene added more hot water to the tub and began to plan the tale she'd weave tonight. Maybe they were on an island, where there was a secret society of men only. He brought her there, introduced her to the Dom, and instructed her to obey whatever orders were given to her. He sat with other men in conversation, drinking brandy and enjoying her humiliation as she performed whatever was asked of her.

~~~

I could tell when I first saw her at the bar— she had money. She could help me with my plan. Ever since I was a kid I'd wanted to make movies, you know those great westerns, with Gary Cooper. Once, years ago, I got a hold of an old eight-millimeter camera, and fooled around with it with my buddies and a girl I was going with at the time. But that was as far as it went. For years, these scenes would run through my head, sometimes Sci-Fi, sometimes westerns, but I was always thinking up the greatest plots.

I never had the money, though. Carpenters don't make enough to fulfill any dreams like that. I had to find somebody with deep pockets. When I met Charlene, my appetite got real intense. Of course, I didn't say anything right away. I had to work up to it. Let her know I liked her as a person, and this was something we could go into together. I knew she'd get a kick out of it.

I'd seen her maybe a dozen times before I said anything. When I did she got all excited, and we made up this story together, just lying in her bed. My dream was finally coming true. The first story we made up was about me, actually, how this man needed money to make a film, and how this rich lady came to his aid, and put up the dough for it. I call these stories scripts, but in the beginning, we never wrote anything down, just had fun doing it out loud.

I didn't feel like I'd be taking advantage of her, either. What was she going to do with all that money? She asked if she could be in the film, and of course I said yes. I was so excited and she sure got in the spirit.

I started writing things down when I got home— story ideas. And then scenes. I brought them to her and asked what she thought. She never made fun of them, but she'd point out where there could be more humor or tension. And conflict, she was always talking about how a book or movie had to have conflict. She was right. We'd act a scene out with her ideas, and then I'd go home and write it down.

We had a good relationship— well rounded. We had great sex and 'playtime' as she called it, She was a great story-teller. And then we had this film preparation. I couldn't wait to get started on the real script.

We always played first. Then after we'd talk about the film. Finally, I said to her one night, "You know I'm gonna need some money for the next step."

She said, "What do you mean?"

"Well, I can't hire a script writer with baseball cards."

She was real quiet.

"What is it?" I said.

"You know we were just play-acting. Having fun making up stories like we were doing all along."

"No, no. Not about the film. You said you'd finance it."

"No, I did not say that."

"You did too! What do you think we've been talking about all this time?"

"Like I said, it was just one of the many scenes we made up for fun, like the others."

"No, it wasn't— it was real!"

"For you, maybe. I'm sorry if you misunderstood."

I started to panic. "Charlene, you gotta help me. I need you. And you'll enjoy it. Give you something to do."

"I enjoy storytelling. But when it comes to what I do with my money, dear boy, that's a whole different ball-game."

"Please, it'll be an investment for you. You'll get your money back."

She got up and put her robe on. "I think you'd better leave."

Suddenly, she was a different person— the fun was over. She was all business.

To save what little pride I had left, I got dressed and walked to the door.

My parting words, "You think it over."

~~~

Brutus arrived late, as usual. That was his style, so Charlene was not surprised, and didn't let it upset her. She'd seen him a couple of times since their argument about financing his film. He hadn't brought it up and neither had she. He hadn't asked her to do any kind of story-telling. She figured he'd accepted reality and let it go.

When he arrived on this night he remained several feet from her, taking in her appearance, her obvious anticipation. Charlene could feel her pulse racing as he just stood there. Was he pleased with what he saw? Had she worn the right gown? She wondered what the expression on her face conveyed to him.

Finally, he said, "Take it all off."

Dismay crossed her face briefly before she willed herself into submission.

Doing as she was told she faced him again, waiting while he appraised her. Her years were beginning to show, but for her age she knew she looked damned good.

"Turn around."

She did.

Was that an angry look on his face?

"Go to the bedroom."

She obeyed.

No simple overtures this time. Not even time to enjoy the wine she'd decanted. Well, maybe later.

He picked up the braided long tail and followed her into the bedroom.

He was very rough that night, rougher than she liked it. She asked him to stop, but he continued. Finally, he threw down the whip and asked, "Have you thought it over?"

At first she was baffled— thought what over? Then she remembered. Trying to sit up, he pushed her down.

"If you mean the money, I'm not going to finance your film."

~~~

This was the night, I was sure of it. I got in the gate as someone was leaving. I remembered my sister's room number from when Gwen was with me.

Nobody was around. I took the elevator up from the garage to the fourth floor. Didn't need to pass the desk. Then I walked along the floor until I came to her room. No noises coming from the inside this time. I tried the door. My luck, it wasn't locked. I had a couple of little tools in case it was, but it wasn't, so I turned the handle and let myself inside.

Charlene was sleeping on her stomach. I crept over to the bed and just looked at her for a while. I could hardly see in the dark. She didn't stir. I guess I lost my nerve about making her listen to me, telling what I was going to do to her. I didn't wake her up or turn her over. It was so easy. She was lying on this pillow, and all I had to do was pull it tight around her face while pressing down on her head with my elbow, and count to two hundred. She didn't put up any fight at all. It was almost too easy— an anti-climax, you know what I mean?

But then I just had to look at her, to make sure she was dead. I flipped her over on her back and saw her face.

Oh, shit! Oh no! What had I done?

CHAPTER 17

Agnes hung up the phone at the front desk of *The Haven*. It was the third time she'd rung Charlene Osmund's room. No answer. She called the health center.

"Molly, health center."

"Charlene Osmund hasn't brought her knobin in, and she isn't answering her phone."

"I'll be right up."

Molly Anderson raised her considerable bulk from her desk in the health center with amazing alacrity, and took the elevator to the fourth floor. The unlocked door opened, the sight within causing Molly to tighten every muscle from her toes to her throat. A nurse for thirty years, not much could shock this woman, but she'd never seen the likes of this. Nevertheless, Molly swallowed her alarm, tried to arouse the lady, and took her pulse. Nothing.

The other residents were not told in the morning. When Charlene didn't come to breakfast, a rumor got around that she'd been taken to the hospital.

"I wonder why Charlene didn't show up— "

"I saw an ambulance about six o'clock this morning. Probably Charlene."

"I'll call the hospital," offered Marjorie.

When Paula Wilson called the health center on the lower floor she was told that there was no information about Charlene Osmund at this time.

~~~

Coroner Simon Cole showed Mark Cranson, the body of Charlene Osmund.

"Looks like she was smothered."

Mark said nothing.

"Look at her back." The coroner pulled down the sheet.

"Good God!"

"Yes. Whip marks." Cole said. "And semen. Very recent."

The coroner picked up one of her hands. "Look at the bruising on her wrists."

Mark Cranson felt his asthma coming on. "I don't understand."

"Her wrists were bound with handcuffs."

"Were they found on her?"

"No, they'd been removed," the detective said.

"They were somewhere in the room?"

"No, we found no trace of them."

"Strange. The killer must have taken them with him."

Cole continued. "A task force will have to be called in to take fingerprints in the deceased's room."

All Mark could do was to nod.

Cole's autopsy report later that day began with, "On the nineteenth of June 1967, Charlene Osmund died from suffocation between two and three a.m."

Mark's first order of business was the unpleasant task of notifying next of kin. He found her admission papers in the file drawer. Riffling through them, he finally found the right one. Next of kin— "None," she'd written.

Almost everyone had someone. He double checked and called the health center.

"Please look up Charlene Osmund's chart, and tell me what she put for next of kin."

The call was returned in five minutes.

"She put 'None'," the nurse said.

Mark Cranson groaned. His head was spinning.

Next, the residents would have to be told— at least that the woman had died.

~~~

Gwen didn't have to wait to read the evening paper until she got home. A colleague put one on her desk at two o'clock.

"Is this where your aunt lives?"

Gwen grabbed the paper. The headlines read, "Murder at *The Haven* Retirement Home".

"Oh, my God!" Gwen's hand shot to her mouth.

Quickly, she scanned the article.

"I have to go," she told her friend. Without further ado she picked up her purse, grabbed her jacket, and flew out the door.

On the drive across the bridge she kept thinking, if any good could have come from the time she was Sonny's hostage, it should have been that she could have helped prevent the death of Charlene Osmund. She'd known what he wanted to do. Mark and the police knew. And no one could stop him.

It was nearing the end of the day, and the road was full of commuters leaving San Francisco for homes in Marin. Driving north, Gwen was impatient, listening to a news program on the radio. Nothing was said about the murder yet.

As she approached the front door of *The Haven* Retirement Home she was met by a policeman.

"No visitors tonight," he informed her.

"But I must see my friend," she protested.

"Only next of kin."

She drove to the nearest public phone and called Megan.

Megan answered the phone in a soft voice.

"It's me, Megan. I was there at the door, but they wouldn't let me in."

"Oh, my. They've really bumped up security this time. You know what happened here, don't you?"

"Yes. They're saying no one can enter— 'next of kin only.'"

"Well, you are my next of kin. I don't have any other."

"Megan, can you call Mark and ask him to let me in? I really want to come up."

"Where are you?"

"At a public phone by the grocery store."

"I'll try. What's the number on the call box?"

Megan gave it to her. "Call me right back."

She waited, shivering by the call box, wishing she'd worn gloves, and a scarf on her head. The wind was really up tonight, pushing saplings almost to the ground. It was scary. Strange weather for June. A police car raced by with its flashing lights heralding its presence.

Finally, the phone in the box rang through from Megan.

"Gwen, is that you?"

"Yes."

"I'm sorry it took so long. I couldn't reach him right away. But yes, he said he'd tell the policeman to let you in."

Gwen had to show ID when she reached the front door of *The Haven*.

The halls were eerily empty as she approached the elevator and walked the length of the fourth floor.

Normally, Gwen would just open the door and say 'Hello.' Tonight it was locked.

"It's me," she called from the hall.

Megan came to the door and opened it. As soon as Gwen was in Megan locked it again.

"Orders," she said. "We're all to keep our doors locked."

"Are you frightened?" Gwen asked.

"Well, of course I am. I never planned to move to a place where my neighbors were being killed. I'm very upset about Charlene. She welcomed me when I first came, and we remained friendly."

"Isn't she the one who made all the noise you didn't like?"

"Well yes. I can't say I enjoyed her nocturnal activities. But I can't imagine who'd want to kill her. She was nice to everyone."

"Did she have any relatives around here?"

"Why would a relative kill her?"

"It happens. Maybe for money. Did she have a lot?"

"Oh, yes. She was one of the wealthiest residents here."

"If it were something like that, I imagine he's long gone, and no one else has anything to worry about," Gwen said.

"Well, you may be right. But we can't assume that," Megan said with emphasis.

"What else do you know about the case?"

Megan shook her head. "Nothing."

"They haven't apprehended anyone?"

"Not that I know of." Megan took a deep breath. "You shouldn't have come, Gwen. You have a busy life, and the people here will take care of this."

Gwen made Megan and herself a cup of tea, and found some ice-cream in the freezer. After discussing the awful event for a while, they moved on to other topics. She was glad Aunt Megan was handling it so well. She had remained calm and peaceful. Then she thought, *Maybe it wasn't Sonny after all.*

On her way home that night she wondered what it was that made her want to dig into these murders, as she had when her friend in Sausalito had been killed. Probably because Megan was here. But was that all it was?

~~~

Denise stopped by to pick up some clothes, and after hearing Denise's news, Gwen couldn't hold it in. She spilled everything she knew to her friend.

"From what I've told you, who do you think was the killer, Denise?"

"I'd say it's the boyfriend. He had the semen, the wrist restraints, and was known to beat her. What for, if not her money?" Denise said.

"I understand she enjoyed it. What about Sonny? He was bent on killing her."

"Would he have used those methods?"

Gwen made a face. "I don't know. He really had it in for her."

Denise shook her head. "Poor lady."

~~~

At breakfast Peggy Sue told the women she sat with that Charlene Osmund had died.

"Died! How?"

"But she'd been healthy!" Alice Tilly said.

"Some of the girls said they thought she had cancer," countered Marjorie.

"She never complained about anything," said Alice, showering the tablecloth with tidbits from her mouth.

Megan said nothing.

"No. Not like some of the girls who give an organ recital at every meal," Paula spoke slowly in her Georgia drawl.

Arlene said, "I used to give piano recitals."

"She wouldn't have wanted sympathy, not Charlene," Marjorie said.

"She was so young— still in her sixties," Gertrude said.

"What did she die of?" Ruth Swanson cried out.

"She died of murder," Peggy Sue said calmly.

A chorus rose of "Oh no,"

"Are you sure?"

"How could that be?"

"I don't believe it."

Peggy Sue declared, "Police are all over the building. They don't come if it's a death of natural cause. If you'd pay attention to what's going on right under your nose, you'd have figured that out."

It was true that most of the residents, seeing police, knew something was wrong. Soon word had spread that there'd been a murder.

"My God, who could have done that?" Alice wondered.

"Is that lunatic still around?" Marjorie said.

"I'm moving out!" Gertrude declared.

~~~

Although the occupants of *The Haven* were mostly women, there was a scattering of married couples, and a few single men. Some were known to have special friends on the outside. One had been Charlene. Although no one seemed to know his name, his face was familiar to those who lived on the fourth floor. The guest book was searched for his name. Three residents helped to go through the list, sure they'd recognize it if they saw it. But no one did.

Upon questioning, the woman who worked the front desk in the evening finally admitted to Mark that this man was such a familiar figure that she didn't require him to sign in. That was strictly against protocol, but that's what Alberta Sawyer, on the evening shift confessed to.

Mark talked to Gwen. They went over and over the facts that they knew, and what they could extrapolate from them.

"There's Sonny, of course. He admitted to me that killing her was his mission."

"Yeah, he's the most likely candidate. But the coroner said that semen was found on Charlene's body. This certainly points to the boyfriend," Mark said. "Was the boy-friend angry with her for a reason?"

"Or, more sinister, had he been seeing her just to get at her money? The old scam," Gwen said.

"Charlene was known to be one of the wealthier women in the retirement home, and her boyfriend was thought to be fifteen to twenty years younger than she. Perhaps she'd refused whatever scheme he'd come up with. First tortur-ing her into turning her stocks and cash over to him, and when that failed, killing her."

It was a possibility. Which man was there that night? Had both come to her room?

With no name it was impossible to trace the boyfriend in police files. An artist was employed to draw a sketch of his face. Several women participated in describing the man to the artist.

"His hair was light brown," offered Alice.

"No," stated Peggy Sue firmly. "It was quite dark and curly. He was ethnic, I'm certain of that."

"I thought his nose rather Patrician," Paula said.

"It was curly," Arlene said.

"Are you kidding? He was as common as fleas," retorted Peggy Sue.

"I only meant his nose," Paula defended.

The poor artist crumpled up several sketches before the women who had seen him came to a more-or-less agree-ment on his image.

The artist said, "Does this one look like him?"

"Kind of."

"Sort of."

An APB was put out with the artist's rendition of the man's facial features. It was also posted in the local news-papers.

At least with the other suspect, they had a name. Sonny Dickens was easy to find in the files. His history, and time spent in Folsom Prison was all there. Folsom provided a photo of him, but nothing they didn't already know. But where was he? An APB was put out on him.

No one came forth.

~~~

I'm back in the fourth-floor trash room, hoping to catch Gwen up here. Dangerous place to be, here so close to the scene of the crime, but it's my best chance.

I found an old newspaper in a trash can. Couldn't help wondering if there was anything in there about me. I never thought I'd be important enough to be in the paper, but there I was, picture and all. Well, that made me feel pretty important, until I realized that now. anyone could recognize me. My heart started beating really fast as I read the article. What surprised me most was according to the paper, it seems they were also looking for some other guy too, but his picture wasn't in the paper. I want to leave this place, but I'm not finished here.

CHAPTER 18

On Monday, Gwen received a letter from the court-appointed lawyer. The notice stated that she, Ms. Anna Reiker would be representing her in court, and that Gwen would be notified soon of a court date.

She could hardly believe it. She wanted to talk to someone about it, and of course, that person was Mark.

She approached his office. It was an awkward moment. He'd been very kind to her, trying to help her avoid that horrible experience, and comforting her afterwards too. But that hadn't changed the fact that he said he was going back to his wife.

Knocking softly on his door, she asked, "May I come in?"

He rose. "Of course. I'm so glad to see you."

Mark motioned for her to sit down.

She told him about the letter.

"This is really bogus," he said. "This is going too far. The guy's a total creep, and you're the one facing charges? It doesn't make sense."

"But what can I do? And just Saturday I got rid of those awful notes he posted on my windshield and front door. I wish I hadn't, now."

"You need a lawyer."

"I have a court-appointed one."

"Are you sure that's going to be good enough?"

"I called a couple others. They charge a fortune. I can't afford it."

He shook his head. "Keep me posted, OK? I'm truly concerned."

She nodded. "The other reason I came was to see if there's anything I can do to help."

"I'd be grateful," he smiled. "We're facing huge pressure, with a second assault."

"No results from the APB?"

He shook his head. "I don't know, Gwen. It's a puzzle all the way around."

He filled his pipe.

"No. Do the residents know how she died?"

"Yes, with all the police around, they know it was foul play. I have to talk to them again. They need to be even more careful. And they don't know this yet, but after a thorough check of all the doors and window openings, the officers have concluded that there was no break-in."

"If it was Sonny I wonder how he got back in."

"He probably knows the building better than I do. Maybe you could help. Charlene died between four and five a.m. But she was seen in the hall around six, according to two witnesses. I'm not ready to challenge the coroner on this point— not yet, anyway."

"You think coroner was wrong about the time of death?"

"Maybe. He might have overlooked something. There are so many factors to consider. Lividity, rigor mortis."

Gwen raised an eyebrow. "Who saw her in the hall?"

"A couple of early risers, going down for coffee. Alice Tipple and Marjorie Hamilton."

"What time was this?"

"About six o'clock."

"Don't things like ambient temperature affect how the time of death is determined?"

"Yes, but we're neither in a Louisiana swamp or an Alaskan glacier. I mean the Coroner Cole's work is always in this temperate climate," Mark said.

Mark rubbed his brow and Gwen could see the whole unsavory business was getting to him.

He seemed to read her mind. "You know, applications from potential residents have already dropped off. And some residents are thinking of moving out. I have to get this thing solved and put the residents at peace."

She wanted to ask him how things were going with his wife. Instead, she said, "What would you like me to do?"

"I thought maybe you could talk to these two women—informally, you know. Listen, find out what they think they saw."

"Hmm."

The next day she arranged with Megan to introduce her to the women who claimed they'd seen Charlene after the time the coroner had established her death.

"Are you sure you want to do this?" Megan said.

"Mark asked me to, and I'm happy to do anything I can to help solve this horrific situation."

Megan nodded. "Let's invite them to lunch."

They waited on a bench in the hall for the women, watching residents proceed to the dining room. As if blown like willows by a western wind, the slow march of those bent over their walkers proceeded to the dining room.

As Alice Tipple and Marjorie Hamilton approached, Megan introduced them to Gwen.

Gwen was careful to steer the conversation away from current events, and not delve too quickly into the particulars.

After asking Gwen about her line of work, where she lived, and so forth, the women brought up the crimes.

"I suppose you know what's been going on here," Alice said.

"Yes, Megan told me. I'm so sorry. It must be very distressing."

"Of course it is," Marjorie added.

"And for all we know, the killer is still among us," Alice said, punctuated by bits of food projected from her mouth.

"We saw Charlene Osmund walking down the hall after the coroner placed her time of death at three or four. He's made a big mistake, because we saw her at six, didn't we Alice?" Marjorie was emphatic.

"Are you sure?"

"Of course, we are," retorted Alice.

Gwen moved her arm. The food particles were coming too close.

They had finished lunch, and were the last ones sitting in the dining room.

Ravinski strode in and approached their table. He was obviously upset.

"I'm Detective Ravinski. You are Alice Tipple and Marjorie Hamilton?"

"Yes," they said simultaneously.

"I'd like to speak with you. But first, I'd like to talk to you, Miss Harris. Would you step over here, please?"

They moved toward the door.

"As you know I am the detective assigned to this case. I don't appreciate your questioning significant members involved."

"Excuse me?" Gwen said in astonishment.

"By talking to these witnesses you may be skewing the truth."

"How so?"

"I need their fresh, honest answers to questions I have. Not some watered-down version of your gossip."

Gwen was offended, but she kept calm.

"I'm sorry, sir. My friend introduced me to them. We were having lunch."

"Yes, and getting information from them, no doubt."

"I was just trying to help."

"You can help by backing off! Leave my witnesses alone!" He was beginning to raise his voice.

"I have Mr. Cranson's permission to talk to the residents."

Arnold Ravinski's face went quickly from pink to red to almost purple.

Gwen smiled. "If you'll excuse me. My aunt and I are ready to leave."

The detective turned and marched out of the dining room. Gwen returned to the table, and summoned Megan.

"What did he say?" Megan wanted to know on the way back to her apartment.

When Gwen told her Megan said, "That's terrible. You're only trying to help."

Gwen felt stymied. If the detective was threatened by her involvement, she didn't know how she could help.

She stopped by Mark Cranson's office and knocked softly on the open door.

He rose from his desk. "Come in. Please do."

He offered her a seat and a weary smile.

Gwen relayed to him her encounter with the two witnesses.

"I'll have to speak with the coroner again. This is very disturbing."

"Is he generally accurate?"

"I imagine he is. But these witnesses are throwing a wrench in the investigation. Making it more confusing than ever." He paused, and played with his empty pipe.

He continued. "Do you think they could have fabricated the story of seeing her later, just to start some mischief? Or that perhaps they were sleep-walking and thought they saw her?" he said.

"They seemed very certain they'd seen her. Adamant, in fact."

"I'll have a talk with them."

"And by the way, the detective thought I was intruding on his turf. Thought I was out of line talking to them."

Mark made a face.

After talking with the two women Mark too, was sure that these two ladies were certain of what they had seen. He placed an immediate call to the coroner.

"I'm sorry to bring this up, but in regard to Charlene Osmund, I was wondering about the time of death— "

"What's to wonder?" snapped the coroner.

"Well, due to two witnesses swearing they saw Charlene several hours after the time that you placed her death— "

The coroner barked, "Are you doubting the veracity of my report?"

"It's just that we would like to reach some concurrence on the time of death."

"You're asking me to change my findings?"

"No sir, not at all." Mark was sweating. "Is there any chance that some unusual factor may have thrown off the obvious conclusion you reached?"

"There were no unusual factors."

"The whip marks— "

"Not a factor in her death. And that's all I have to say."

Mark heard the phone click. Well, that was a dead end. What did he mean 'not a factor in her death'? Well, he realized that those marks didn't indicate the time that she died. Of course, the coroner was right about that.

As to the disparity between the accounts, this part of the tragedy was inexplicable— at least for now.

CHAPTER 19

The next morning Ravinski walked into Mark's office without knocking. He wanted to see the cleaning lady who'd been assigned to Charlene's room. Mark called her up, and she was brought into his office where the detective stood over her.

"When was the last day that you cleaned Miss Dickens' room?"

The girl twisted her hands, and sent a pleading eye toward Mark.

Mark said, "Not to worry, Lorena, you're not in trouble. Just answer the detective's questions."

The girl chewed her lip before she mumbled, "The day before she died."

"I didn't hear that."

She cleared her throat and tried again.

"The day before she died."

"Did you notice anything unusual at that time?"

"No, sir."

"Did you at any time, see or hear anything that struck you as strange?"

With her eyes glued to her lap, she shook her head.

Ravinski exchanged glances with Mark, and then pressed on.

"You must tell the truth, Loraine. We're talking about a murder."

The girl began to weep, and looked toward the door.

"Can I go now?"

Mark cut in. "Yes, for now."

Lorena all but ran out of the office.

"Why did you let her go?" Ravinski demanded. "She's hiding something."

"You're probably right. But this wasn't going anywhere. Let me handle it."

"For God's sake, man, this is police work!"

"I'm aware of that."

"What do you intend to do? Bring in your assistant again?"

"Perhaps. The girl's frightened to death. In any case, she needs to talk to someone who can win her trust."

Ravinski grunted. "You want my help, and then you dismiss my witnesses."

"Sorry. We're not all suited for all roles. I just think this time— "

"Now you're schooling me on police work!"

"No, sir. I'm merely pointing out— "

Ravinski stormed out of the office, and out of the building.

~~~

Police officers were crawling all over the retirement home. Maintenance, kitchen and housekeeping staffs were being interviewed one at a time in the auditorium, the library, and the social room.

Quiet whispers were heard in the dining room. The staff was nervous too. Twice, the clatter of dropped plates was heard, violating the hush, and raising tension further.

And how was Barbara involved? Was she just an unfortunate sidebar to the killer's agenda? Or was she a target in her own right?

~~~

Working next to Dick got more and more difficult. He openly jeered at her for playing detective and after three days, having found no suspects.

"A great journalist you are— not a single article for the paper. Nada. While you're playing amateur detective across the bridge, all we have here is a teeny bit on the back page stating that the police have been unable to take any steps toward arresting the perp."

Gwen struggled hard to resist answering back. It wouldn't do any good; he'd know he'd gotten her goat. He must know that writing up the murder was not in her jurisdiction.

She wrote something about the new building going up on Market Street, and worked on the Society page about the Junior League women funding a charity event at the Fairmont Hotel. How she wished she could write about the subject she knew most about.

When she got home, there was another letter from the court. This time it was signed by a different attorney, summoning her to court on the fifteenth of July. What was going on? She called the legal department.

"This is not unusual," he was told. "Ms. Reiker's load was probably too big."

She tried to reach her new attorney by phone. He didn't answer. He didn't return her calls.

Three days later she went to the Public Defender's office and asked to see him. He did come out of his office, but stood there in the busy lobby, requiring she address her question to him there.

When she asked why he didn't return her call, he said, "Because I have two hundred cases."

"I'd like to know if you received a copy of the letter I wrote to the expeditor."

"No, I don't have your file yet."

"Is there a time we can review my case before the court date?"

"What is it you want to discuss?"

She took a deep breath. "I think the case should be dismissed. I explained it all in my letter."

"I'll call you if the file's passed on to me." He turned to leave.

"Please do."

Gwen was ready to scream.

~~~

A memorial service for Charlene was being held on Saturday. Gwen sat beside her aunt. It was unusually hot for June, especially in the auditorium, which held not a single fan, nor was it air-conditioned.

"I think it's in the nineties," Paula remarked, who had thought to bring a paper fan.

"Eighty-three," Peggy Sue corrected.

"No circulation of air at all," Paula added, swishing her fan vigorously.

While they were waiting, residents talked in lowered voices.

"I saw Victor with another woman last night," Peggy Sue said. "You know my window overlooks the back stairs. He sneaked her in that way."

"Who was she?"

"No one we know. She's not from here. She had flaming red hair."

"Are you going to tell Ruth?"

"Heavens no."

"I'm going to say something to the cook," announced Alice. "We had chicken for dinner last night and again this noon."

"And spaghetti twice on Wednesday," added Marjorie. "I don't care what she calls it, it's still spaghetti!"

As Gwen surmised, no family members were there. Sonny had told her that both their parents were deceased.

A non-denominational minister was called in to give the service, although no one could recall if Charlene ever attended any church. Mark had seen to it that flowers were brought in and placed on the stage. Other flower arrangements were given by some of the residents. Later they would be placed in common areas of the home.

The minister began by speaking of the terrible tragedy, the hope that justice would be done, and that the perpetrator would find forgiveness from God. In order to personalize the eulogy, residents, including Megan, had given the pastor information about the woman—things she'd done for others, like visiting residents in the health center, and setting up a fund for those who might run out of money.

"When's the wedding going to start?" asked Arlene. "I don't see the bride."

Paula fell asleep. Peggy Sue jerked her arm forcefully. She woke up with a loud snort.

The projection booth, high above, was in the back of the auditorium. While soft music played, slides were shown of the few pictures taken of Charlene during various functions at *The Haven.*

Someone in the back was snoring. Purses were heard snapping open and shut as women reached for their handkerchiefs. The photos had touched them more than the words. The service concluded with the playing of an LP record of *Nearer My God to Thee.* However, the needle stuck in a groove, and the phrase *My God* repeated over and over until the needle was taken off the record, rendering a macabre finish to the service.

~~~

Gwen continued meeting small groups on each floor, some residents on a one-to-one. They wanted to talk about their fear that the murderer might come back, how they couldn't sleep or had nightmares. But mostly they were hoping for fresh news as to any developments in finding the killer. Gwen had to be honest— the police were working on it, but no, no new developments. The best she could do was to commiserate with them, let them get their feelings out.

On Tuesday morning when she talked to the two women who claimed to have seen the victim the night after the coroner's recorded time of death, they held fast to their belief that Charlene had, in fact, been in the hall at six o'clock, and therefore the coroner was wrong. Gwen believed they were telling the truth— at least their truth. She was sure they weren't lying. They were highly offended when it was suggested that they might have been walking in their sleep.

Later that morning Gwen met with a group on the first floor, while Mark was seeing those who wished to speak privately in his office. A woman in the back raised her hand, and Gwen called on her above the chatter.

"You said they were still seeking the killer. Haven't they arrested anyone yet?"

"No, they haven't."

Shouts went up.

"What!"

"Why?"

"Who would do such a thing?"

"What about fingerprints?"

Gwen signaled for silence.

Disgruntled sounds erupted. One voice came through loud and clear.

"What about Alice and Marjorie, who saw her walking the hall after she was supposedly dead?"

"Mr. Cranson is looking into that."

A groan.

"They swear they saw her. Could the coroner have gotten the time of death wrong?"

"These things are being explored." Gwen took a deep breath. "You're asking important questions. I don't have the answers, but I am here to listen to your concerns. And I will pass them on to Mr. Cranson."

A few more queries and Gwen brought the meeting to a close, promising she'd be available three evenings a week if they wanted to talk.

"It's doubtful that the perpetrator would still be hanging around the building. I urge caution, but I don't think you need to live in fear."

As she left the room Gwen didn't feel she'd done anything to allay their fears. She felt totally inept in this job. And the last question struck her mind like a loud bell, demanding answers. What indeed was the significance of the witnesses who claimed they'd seen the murdered woman hours after the coroner had declared her death? Were they sleep walking, deliberately making it up, or was the coroner wrong?

Well, she wasn't hired to solve this problem.

She stopped in Mark's office to tell him how things had gone. He suggested they go to lunch together.

"Not here," he said. "Too many prying eyes and ears. You can give me your report over lunch."

Gwen agreed, and they drove down 101 to Sausalito, parked on Bridgeway and entered the Trident restaurant. She felt a welcome relief from the heat wave as they entered. Much cooler here on the water than in San Rafael. They were led to a booth in the back, and at one-thirty, the eatery was half empty.

"The Kingston Trios started this restaurant," Gwen said.

"I didn't know that. Have you ever seen them?"

"Once. Some of us from *The Chronicle* were invited to a performance here."

"Bonuses a reporter gets, huh?"

"Friend of a higher ranking journalist," she smiled.

"So, what do you have to tell me— what are 'the girls' saying?"

"Not a lot. Nothing that would surprise you. Everyone's on edge, suspicious— even angry that no one's been arrested. They think it's the boyfriend. Of course, they're biased, because they've seen him, and have never seen Sonny."

Mark shook his head. "We're still trying to locate him. Personally, I don't think the boyfriend's our bad boy."

"I don't either," she said thinking of Sonny.

"Listen, I have an idea. It's unlikely there will be any more murders. Let's plan a fun evening, thank the residents and staff for their patience during this trying time, which is now over. We can make it really festive— have some music, clear part of the auditorium floor for dancing, and serve refreshments. What do you think?"

He was talking about *The Haven*, but there was something in his expression that made her feel he was musing about something else.

"I think it's a great idea."

"How about next Saturday? We'll call it 'Dance Tonight!' Evening events don't attract many people, and the staff wants to go home, so let's make it three o'clock."

Their seafood salad arrived, and they both stopped talking as they ate with relish.

When they'd finished, Mark folded his arms on the table and looked Gwen straight in the eye.

"It was a mistake," he said.

Gwen thought he meant taking her to lunch.

"Going back with Marlene. I should have known it wouldn't work. By the second night I knew that. I'm back sleeping in my office."

"I'm sorry," Gwen mumbled.

"I don't know how you feel, after I ended it with you like I did, but, well. . ."

He started coughing, and looked away.

Gwen waited.

He took her hand. "I love you, Gwen. I want to be with you . . . if you'll have me."

She was happy. She was even thrilled. But all she did was smile. She wasn't going to jump in his lap and lick his face like a puppy.

"Think about it."

"I will."

CHAPTER 20

The June heat wave was over, and cool breezes came in to take its place. Plans were being made for the Saturday party.

Mark assumed that Gwen would want to be involved, and she was glad to accommodate. They shopped for party favors, colorful paper napkins, snacks and drinks. Mostly soft drinks, but Gwen convinced Mark that a flavored punch would be a nice alternative.

"And what flavor would that be?" he smiled.

"Rum. I have a good recipe. And a punch also."

"Let's do it."

Invitations were sent out, and the response was very positive.

A strobe light was attached to the ceiling, and colorful balloons were placed everywhere.

The afternoon of the party Mark and Gwen had fun in the kitchen mixing the punch, tasting it, and preparing the snacks. Card tables with colorful cloths had been placed by the housekeeping staff.

"I'll play bar tender," Mark announced.

"I'll circulate, making sure everyone has what they need," Gwen said.

"Did I tell you about the band?"

"No."

"Some of the residents formed a little group called *Gus and the Guys.* They agreed to do some numbers, so that will put a final polish on our party."

"Splendid."

At three o'clock promptly, residents started filing in. Mostly women and mostly glad for an occasion to dress up, they looked expectant. Three members of the band were tuning up. Pretty soon, more ladies arrived, all swathed in long gowns, some even with fur pieces. The atmosphere was convivial for a change. Drinks were served, and people sat chatting around the tables.

Three men walked in and sat together at a far table.

"I wish they'd spread out among the women," Paula said. "They hang together like the boys in junior high did."

"Those two guys who just walked in are bachelors. New on our floor," Gertrude said.

"Yes, one is deaf, and the other blind," Paula said.

Not to be discouraged by the lack of a man or lack of full mobility, a woman who called herself Chartreuse was out on the floor kicking up a storm by herself with her walker.

"Wow, that takes courage," Megan said.

Ruth waltzed in on the arm of Victor.

A man wearing overalls and an old plaid shirt sauntered in across the floor. The girls rolled their eyes.

"He can't even wear decent clothes for a special party," Gertrude said. "And they say he's loaded."

"I never saw his gun," Arlene said.

"He looks like an unmade bed," added Alice with a drool.

The girls started talking about how they used to love to go dancing with their husbands, naming the places they'd been. That led to what kind of careers the husbands had.

"Claude began the wallpaper company in St. Louis. It's still there."

"My husband had that huge cereal factory in Battle Creek," said Gertrude.

"Which one?" asked Paula. "There are two."

Gertrude waved her off. "I don't know. That was a long time ago."

Paula turned to Peggy Sue. "I don't believe you ever told us what your husband did."

Peggy Sue raised her head and fingered one of her diamond earrings. "I never really knew. But he did it very well." She glowed.

Gwen was looking at the band members who were sitting in silence on the stage.

"I wonder why the band doesn't start playing," she said to Mark.

"I'll go see."

He was back in a few moments.

"It seems Gus hadn't shown up. I told them to go ahead and play something until he comes."

Mark approached Charlie, who he knew occupied the apartment next to Gus's.

"Go see if you can rustle him up," he said.

The three members of the group began to play *I Want to Hold Your Hand.*

Without their leader, the piano player, they sounded a little thin. Peggy Sue went up to them.

"Where's Gus?"

"Somebody went to fetch him. Maybe he fell asleep," the bass player said.

After fifteen minutes Charlie returned. "Couldn't find him anywhere. His door was open, so finally I just went in. No Gus. I looked in his usual hangouts in case he forgot— the pool room, the library— nothing."

Gwen looked at Mark. "What do you think happened?"

"Don't know."

Gwen thought he looked worried.

Peggy Sue, Paula and Ruth approached.

"Why don't we have Gus today?" Ruth asked.

"I'm sure he'll be along," Mark said.

"Well, something must be wrong," Paula said. "Gus is very reliable. He wouldn't just not show up."

"Maybe he's at the dentist, getting his hearing aids," Arlene offered.

"Peggy Sue confronted Mark. "Someone should look for him. Something might have happened to him."

Mark swallowed. He didn't want fearful rumors to spread.

"We're looking into it. Go enjoy your punch, ladies."

But Gwen saw the women separate, as each visited a different table.

"Stirring up trouble," Gwen said. "Damn, their igniting fear again."

She could see the look of consternation on the faces of those being informed of Gus's absence.

"They're probably telling everyone there's been another murder," Mark said. "I should go look for him myself."

"If you leave, they'll know something's wrong."

"You're right."

"I'll go," Gwen said.

"No. No, please don't. It could be dangerous— " Mark said.

"You don't really think. . ."

"I don't know what to think. Listen, why don't you go to the office and call Mario in maintenance. Tell him to look in every conceivable place for Gus— closets, everything."

As she was leaving the room someone screamed. Gwen turned back and saw a huddle of people bending over something or someone.

It was Paula. She lay on the floor in agony.

Gwen asked, "What happened?"

Someone said, "She fell."

Well, that was obvious.

"The floor was wet— spilled drink, I guess," Megan said.

"It's the punch— someone spiked the punch. I could tell she was drunk," Peggy Sue shouted.

Mark approached. "No, don't try to move her," he called to the two men trying to raise her. "We'll call the health center."

"I'll go," Gwen said.

The crowd started to thin out. The band stopped playing, the fun was over. Again, anxious faces surrounded them.

Gwen went to the office and called the health center. Then she called Mario in maintenance to search for Gus.

Help arrived from the health center, and lifted Paula onto a gurney.

In silence, Gwen and Mark began to clean up after the party. Two helpful ladies came to their assistance, clearing drinks and snack plates from the tables.

As they left, one said, "It was a nice party, Mr. Cranson. We know you did a lot to cheer us up."

When they'd gone, Mark broke the silence. "Well, that was a fiasco, wasn't it?"

"I don't think everyone thought so. It was almost time for the party to end anyway." Gwen said.

"I'm going to find Gus, if it's the last thing I do," Mark said.

"And I'll go see how Paula's doing."

Gwen returned from the health center and stopped in to see her aunt.

"Are you OK?" she asked.

"Fine. Tired, but fine."

"What was the gossip?"

"Well, the girls are at it again— you know, spreading rumors that the murderer is still here, what with Gus missing. Lots of criticism about the rum in the punch. They blamed that for Paula's fall."

"I just went down to see how she was doing. They think she has a broken hip, so she's been taken to the hospital," Gwen said.

"Anyone could have fallen on that wet spot. I don't think she had any punch," Megan said.

"I hate to run, but I want to see if Mark found Gus."

"Oh, go along. But let me know, will you?"

"Of course."

She headed for the first floor. She ran into Mark in the hall outside his office.

"I was about to go hunting for you," he said.

"Did you find Gus?"

"Yes, finally. Poor guy was stuck in his bathtub."

"Bathtub!"

"Yeah, he's ninety-two, you know, and he usually takes showers. But today he wanted a bath, and when it came time to get out, he didn't have the strength."

"Oh, how awful."

"I helped him into bed. He was freezing."

"Why didn't he drain some water and keep adding hot?"

"I don't know. Didn't think of it, I guess. He said he tried to raise himself over and over, but he just couldn't."

"Poor guy. Is he OK now?"

"I think so. I called health service and asked them to check on him. Gus says he heard Charlie come in, but he couldn't make himself heard when he called out over the music playing in the living room. His bathroom door was shut, and Charlie didn't go in there."

"Oh, my God. You'd think that's the first place he'd look."

"Yeah." Mark wiped his forehead with his handkerchief. "What did you find out about Paula— how's she doing?"

"She's at the hospital. They think she broke her hip."

Mark just shook his head. He took Gwen's hands. They both took a deep breath.

"May I take you to dinner?"

Gwen shook her head. "It's my turn. I'll whip up some-thing at home."

"But you're tired."

"Leftovers."

"OK."

While they ate, although they tried not to, the conversa-tion kept returning to the failure of the party.

"Well, we tried," Mark said.

"Yes, we did. Now let's put that behind us for a while."

"Fine with me," he smiled.

He turned toward her. "Have you thought about what I said— before?"

Gwen took a few moments to answer. "Yes. I have to admit it hurt when you ended it. I'm feeling more cautious now. I don't want to go through that again."

"I promise, you won't."

"It will just take time, Mark. I'm not ready to jump in where we left off."

He sighed. "I understand."

"I'm just too gullible. I have to learn to curb my emotions."

"I wish you wouldn't."

~~~

I've been casing the basement. There's some rooms off the garage. Most of them are locked, but I found one that isn't. I call it the pipe room, cuz it's full of big pipes going up and down, and sideways. I guess it's the boiler room, hotter than hell.

I can't leave yet, gotta get Gwen to help me. All this waiting around, I'm stuck here with my memories again. I'm kind of reliving that fatal night, that put me in prison for thirty-five years. I can't help it. Thirty-five fucking years, and the reason I have to do what I'm going to do tonight. I remember it like it was yesterday, because I remembered it every day in prison. It's branded on my mind.

CHAPTER 21

The phone rang early the next morning.

"Gwen, it's Megan. I tried to reach you at work, but they said you weren't in."

"What's going on?"

"I need to talk to you. Can I come over?"

"I'll come to you, Megan."

"No, not here."

"Then let's meet at that little park near you."

What could be wrong? More trouble at *The Haven*?

Gwen drove north, then west toward *The Haven*. Before getting to *The Haven*, she turned left into a little park. and drove down the dirt that passed for a parking lot. Sauntering over the grass she found a bench to sit on. After waiting ten minutes for Megan, her aunt arrived, pale and weak.

Plopping down onto a bench she said, "I need water."

Megan took a small bottle from her purse and downed its contents.

Gwen was worried now that Megan was either sick or had had a bad fright. She waited while the older woman took some deep breaths.

"What I'm about to tell you, you can't laugh, and you can't tell anyone else. Understand?"

"I won't laugh. I don't know about telling— it depends."

Megan made a sour face, but she went on. "I was walking down the hall last night. I get these cramps in my legs— they wake me up and I can't sleep. My legs keep jerking. The only thing for it is to walk. It's happened lots of time before, and I walk back and forth down the hall.

After what happened, I know I shouldn't have. But I did last night."

Gwen drew in her breath. "Go on."

"This is the part you won't believe."

"Tell me."

Megan leaned over closely to Gwen, making sure no one was in ear shot, and whispered. "I saw the ghost of Charlene last night. I know it sounds crazy, I knew you wouldn't believe me. And you don't. I can tell by your face."

"I'm not dismissing anything. I'm sure you saw something. Can you describe what you saw?"

"It looked just like her, then it darted into the laundry room. I just went right back to my room as fast as I could."

"Had you been asleep before your legs started jerking?"

"Yes. Why? But I didn't get any sleep after that."

Gwen didn't know how to phrase it without being offensive. Megan did it for her.

"You think I was sleep walking, don't you?"

"You might have been sleepy— "

"And imagined it! I might have known. Nobody will believe it." She snatched up her purse.

"What was she wearing?"

"Something green. I'd never seen it before."

Gwen had another thought, but didn't think it was time to voice it.

"I'll look into it. I promise," she said, placing her hand over Megan's.

As she drove to work Gwen's thoughts kept returning to the question: Was Sonny still around? If so, why?

Something was niggling in the wings of her mind. She couldn't bring it center stage. Something about the ghost. But what was it? By the time she got to work she knew.

That evening Gwen arrived at *The Haven* at six o'clock.

"Mark, I need to talk to you about something Megan told me."

He gave her a brief kiss. "Good. Tell me what's on your mind."

"I thought you should know. Megan called me in the morning and we met at the park near here. She was scared and didn't want to meet here. Anyway, what she told me was that she saw the ghost of Charlene."

A resounding squeal from Mark's chair punctuated Gwen's pronouncement, as he swiveled front and center.

"Now, unless you believe in ghosts," Gwen continued, "something's going on that needs looking into."

"Jesus!"

"We have to take this apparition seriously. Megan is not one to fantasize ghosts."

"What do you think?"

"To begin with, I don't think Sonny has left the grounds."

"No?"

"I think Sonny is the ghost."

Mark let out a low whistle. "But he already killed Charlene. Or someone did."

"I know. But he is Charlene's sister, and that would explain the likeness, and why three people now, believe they saw Charlene or her ghost."

"Why's he still here?"

"I don't know, but he must be."

"I never got a look at him," Mark said. "Only prison shots."

"He's medium build, brown hair turning gray." She smiled. "Lovely dark eyes."

"You were attracted to him?"

"No. There is some resemblance between them. Charlene wore her hair short, so does he. And did you notice in the pictures they showed at her service? She was always dressed like a man."

"Pants, you mean?"

"Yes. It's the only thing that would explain the ghost," she said.

"Why would he still hang around?"

"I don't know."

"Oh, my God."

Mark rubbed his forehead. "Let me think." He stood up, pacing the room. "Charlene was handcuffed— you think her brother did that? She was whipped, and then smothered with a pillow." His look conveyed his disbelief.

Gwen shrugged. "I know. But can you think of a better explanation of these 'sightings' by the women?"

"No, I can't. Did Megan think this 'ghost' was larger than his sister?"

"She didn't say, but I don't think so. She must have been taken by surprise."

Let me think a minute. First Barbara was knocked out and dumped down the chute. You think he did that? Did he tell you he did that?"

"No, but why would he tell me?"

They chewed on this a while, and then Mark said, "Now I have a puzzle for you."

"What's that?"

Coroner Cole called yesterday and said he'd been studying some pictures of Charlene that he'd taken the day of her death."

"And?"

"According to the bruises made from the handcuffs, it looks like she was turned over and the handcuffs reapplied."

"What? Why?"

"It's all too bizarre.

"How can he tell?"

"According to Cole the biggest bruise is where the handcuffs fasten — any handcuffs if they're tight. And each wrist had two bruises opposite each other."

"Which means?"

"He thought she'd been turned over, and the handcuffs reapplied. He didn't offer any theory as to why."

"What do you make of it?"

"Perhaps she was threatened."

"She was already being hurt."

"Threatened with death," Mark said.

"Which she got anyway."

They stopped talking, each in a private whirlwind of possible scenarios.

"Why bother to whip someone if you're going to murder them?" Gwen said.

"Vengeance?"

"Maybe murder wasn't the original intention."

Mark sighed. "All conjecture. I have to tell Ravinski about what your aunt saw, and about this new theory—that the culprit is Charlene's twin."

"She didn't want me to tell anyone."

"She wants the murderer caught, doesn't she?" He took her hand. "I really appreciate your coming in to share this information with me."

"I don't think Megan would."

No one had seen a stranger on an elevator, so Mark decided that this 'ghost' which had been seen on different floors, had to be using the stairs. He stationed the uniformed cop that Ravinski had provided to patrol the stairways. There were three officers, taking shifts one at a time. They covered all floors, including the basement, and the three sets of stairs.

When three days went by, and no one was seen on the stairs, Ravinski ordered a special dust to be sprayed on them. It would allow them to detect foot prints later. The residents were told to use elevators only.

But in the following days no footprints were found on any of the stairways. How was this mad man getting from floor to floor?

~~~

Mark wanted Gwen to talk to the maid Lorena. The girl seemed to be hiding something, and he thought Gwen was the best person to get the truth out of the girl.

With Gwen in his office, he sent for the cleaning lady. Her face expressed the same fear as it had before.

"Lorena," Mark said, "This is Miss Harris. She's been helping our residents deal with the awful tragedies here, and I thought she would be a good one for you to talk to."

Mark smiled and left the room.

Gwen opened a coke, and poured it in two glasses. She offered one to Lorena.

The girl shook her head. Gwen held hers, and put the other on the table. "In case you change your mind."

"Please sit down, Lorena. I've listened to many of the residents here. I'd like to listen to you, too."

Lorena sat down, but shook her head. "I got nothing to say," she murmured.

"When was the last time you were in Miss Osmund's room?"

"I cleaned it the day before she died."

"I know. But when was the last time you were in her room?"

"I don't know anything. I didn't do nothing wrong!"

"I'm sure you didn't. No one is accusing you of anything. Do you understand that, Lorena?"

The girl looked up briefly, then down at her lap.

"We know there's something you're not telling us. Perhaps something very important. But we won't know until you do tell us."

"Promised not to."

"A promise you made to Miss Osmund?"

"Yes, ma'am."

"I admire you for keeping a promise, Lorena, but she's dead now. Whatever promise you made to Miss Osmund when she was alive, is no longer valid. You can tell me. I think that will lift a big burden off your shoulders."

The girl remained silent. She allowed her lustrous black hair to fall over her face.

Gwen said quietly, "You can tell me, or you can tell the detective at the police station."

Suddenly, Lorena picked up the coke and took a couple of gulps. Still twisting the glass in her hands, she looked imploringly at Gwen.

"Promise you won't tell?"

"I can't promise you that, dear. But you aren't in any trouble; I can promise that."

Lorena quickly finished her coke. "She had me do stuff for her."

"What kind of stuff?"

The girl lifted her glass before realizing it was empty.

"Here, have mine. I haven't touched it."

Lorena accepted it. Sipped it slowly, thinking.

"When she was expecting that man, she'd have me get her these things."

"What kind of things?"

The girl gulped down the rest of the coke.

"Just tell me, in a general way, what sort of things did you do for Miss Osmund?"

"I'd get her toys. She called them toys."

"What kind of toys?"

The girl squirmed. "Whips and things."

"Where did you get them?"

"In her locker, in the basement."

"She gave you the key?"

"Yes."

"And you did this for her often?"

"Every time she asked me to."

"And did you also put these things away when she was finished with them?"

"Yes, the next morning, early while she was still sleeping. They'd be spread out all over the floor in her bedroom. I had to pick them up and put them back in the bag. A zipped up bag."

"And take them back to the locker?"

"Yes."

"Do you still have the key?"

Lorena fished it out of her pocket and gave it to Gwen.

"And a key to her apartment?"

"Yes, to all the apartments I clean."

"Did Miss Osmund pay you to do this for her?"

The girl started to cry. "Yes," she mumbled. "We're not supposed to take tips or presents or anything from them. We get a Christmas bonus."

"Lorena, did you go back to her apartment and pick up the toys the morning after she died?"

The girl looked frightened again.

"It's alright. You can tell me."

Lorena twisted in her chair and bit her lip. She said nothing.

"There is something else, isn't there?"

Gwen opened another coke, and gave it to the girl.

Without pouring it into a glass, Lorena took several long sips, wiped her mouth, and clenched the bottle with both hands.

"You'll feel better if you get it all out. I know you will."

Still the girl said nothing.

Gwen decided to wait patiently until Lorena was ready to talk.

Finally, squirming in her seat, she whispered, "She weren't dead when I saw her."

"Go on."

"It was like always. She told me to pick up the stuff and put it away. Then she turned over and went back to sleep. I knew she was sleeping 'cuz before I left she was snoring."

"She was awake and talking?"

"Yeah."

"What time was that?"

"About six o'clock."

"She didn't seem upset about anything?"

Lorena shook her head.

"Did you see anyone in the halls after you left Miss Osmund's room?"

"No, ma'am."

Gwen smiled, and said, "That's all for now. Thank you for your help, Lorena."

She took the key to Mark and reported what the girl had told her.

"If she's telling the truth, Miss Osmund was still alive when the cleaning lady went in, and Charlene was killed later."

"That would clear the boyfriend and put the blame on Sonny."

"Yup."

"She said she was in there at six o'clock?" Mark whistled. "That's one more conflicting report of when she died."

Gwen could only shake her head.

As they descended to the basement, Mark asked, "Do you know her locker number?"

"Seventy-eight."

When they found Charlene's locker, they had to dig through a lot of other things before they found the zippered bag.

"Guess she didn't want it too visible."

Mark took it out and opened it.

"I don't think we should touch this stuff." But he did look at it and shake his head.

Gwen pulled out a fancy gown in purple satin and chiffon.

"I wonder if she wore this the night she was . . ."

"Let's take it upstairs."

Mark zipped up the bag and they headed back up.

When Ravinski examined the items he said, "If we ever find the suspects, the fingerprints on these items will at least tell us who was using them on the victim."

~~~

That evening Gwen rustled up some leftover chicken and salad, and Mark stopped to buy some wine. Listening to an LP on the turntable, she felt immediately transported to a softer world.

When they'd finished eating, she left the dishes in the sink, and sat with Mark over another glass of Chablis.

After a bit, he put his own glass down and gently did the same with hers.

He met no resistance as he pulled her into his arms. A spark grew to a flame to a full-fledged fire in a matter of seconds.

No resistance on her part. Passion moved them along the route toward the inevitable.

He pulled her up. "Let's find your private venue."

She led him to her room.

A warm evening with no air conditioning and no breeze, beads of sweat were forming on both on them and soaking the sheets.

She broke away and laughed, "I need a fan."

"Yes, you do."

"Do you really sleep in the office?"

"Have been, yes."

"Is it as hot as this?"

"No, but I'm all alone there. You're a furnace." He pulled her back to him.

This time there was no Denise to interrupt them.

Gwen felt the familiar response and heightened by his expertise, her body rose and fell in rhythm with his until both of them lay satisfied in a sea of sweat.

CHAPTER 22

On Thursday, when Gwen picked up her mail after work, the first thing she saw was a letter from the court demanding that she appear in courtroom number six at nine o'clock on the next Tuesday.

When she arrived on the appointed date she asked one of the attending sheriff officers if he could point out her attorney. He did, but the attorney did not approach her.

The judge began by taking attendance of those summoned, and it became apparent that everyone had been called for nine o'clock. Two hours later she was summoned to the front of the room, where it was explained to her that she could sign a declaration of guilt and pay various and sundry charges, and the whole case would be closed today.

She was told that if she declined, a future trial date would be set. Gwen couldn't admit to the charges, so she did not sign.

She left tired and frustrated by the whole procedure, which had taken all morning. She decided to stop and tell Mark about it on the way to work.

He listened sympathetically, and when she said she had to get going to work, he said, "How would you like me to pick you up after work and take you some place special in the city?"

Her mood picked up. "I can't think of anything nicer," she said.

~~~

Mark drove into *The Chronicle* parking lot, knew he was early, and decided to venture inside to see Gwen's working environment. He spotted her across the room that contained many people at as many desks pouring over typewriters. Next to her sat a familiar face. He couldn't believe who it was.

Dick saw him approach and said, "Well if it isn't the Grand Pooh-bah, Mr. Cranson."

Mark stared at him. This was the Dick that had made Gwen miserable for months, and now he knew why. He had fired Dick Jenkins two years before, and the man was taking it out on Gwen. Always a sour, disagreeable man, he'd been hired by Mark's predecessor. After Mark let him go Dick had been hired and fired by the Examiner. How he'd attained work at *The Chronicle* was more than Mark could fathom, unless he had a friend in high places.

Mark refused to engage in conversation. He had all he could do not to grab him by the collar and punch him in the face. That this man had made Gwen miserable was intolerable. Gwen looked nervously from one to the other, put the cover over her typewriter, gathered up her things and rose.

When they reached his car, she said, "What was that all about— do you know him?"

"He used to work at *The Haven* in Finance. I had to fire him, for misallocation of funds. God, I wish I could fire him now."

"You mean he stole money?"

"You could say that. He juggled the accounts and dipped into the coffers."

"Oh, my God! You think that's why— "

"I do." He put his hand over Gwen's. "I'm so sorry. I'm sorry you've taken the brunt of his bitterness toward me."

"Well, at least I know now why he's been so horrid."

Mark had a mischievous smile on his face.

"Where are we going?"

"Be patient."

"Not my strong suit."

"Practice."

She punched him playfully.

Mark took Gwen to a beautiful upscale restaurant called The Blue Fox. They started with the house specialty cocktail, followed by a multi-course dinner which lasted well into the evening.

As they drove home Gwen said, "That was so relaxing. I wish all life could be lived at this pace."

"You'd soon be bored," Mark said.

"You think so? I could take it for quite a while."

"Why do you think people only visit Hawaii, but don't live there?"

"Some do."

"Granted. But most people are content to leave after a week. They need to stay busy."

On the way back to the house Gwen asked, "Did they ever figure out how Sonny was getting around at *The Haven?*

"No. No evidence of him on the elevators or the stairs. But food's been disappearing again, and on at least three of the floors

"How's he getting around? Rappelling the outside walls?"

When they reached Gwen's, they put aside thoughts of *The Haven.* Mark put his arm around her and led her to the bedroom. In the hour that followed a long and lingering love-making took place.

"You'd get tired of this after a week?" Gwen asked.

"Maybe not for two weeks," he teased, starting in all over.

CHAPTER 23

Barbara Kelly had survived, but she'd had a minor stroke, and her speech was coming back slowly. Her doctor was adamant that nothing interfere with her progress. No drama, no trauma to set her back. Anxiously, Ravinski waited for the day the hospital staff would give him permission to question her. Finally, he was allowed in her room accompanied by a woman. That woman was Gwen, who was to do the questioning. It was made clear to the detective that he was there to listen, and if Miss Kelly showed any signs of distress, they were to leave. A nurse was also present.

First, Gwen introduced herself and Ravinski. Then she asked Barbara what she could remember. She left the question open, so that Barbara could run with it in any way that came to her mind.

Haltingly, Barbara spoke, often struggling to find the word she needed, and sometimes trying to remember what she was supposed to be talking about.

Eventually, she did remember getting ready for her trip. With starts and stops she talked quite a while about Ireland and what she planned to do while she was there. Gwen made no attempt to get on with it, even though the detective was coughing and shuffling his feet.

When she finished, Gwen asked, "What is the last thing you remember doing that night?"

Barbara looked confused. Gwen watched the woman thinking. Finally, her face lit up and she said, "I took the garbage to the trash chute."

"And then?"

Barbara looked blank. She scratched her elbow and looked at Gwen for help. She shook her head. "I don't know."

The nurse stood up. "Time for you to go. Enough for today."

When they were in the hall the nurse said, "Traumatic events like she experienced are often hidden deep in the psyche. They may surface eventually, or they may stay buried forever."

As they walked toward the elevator, Ravinski said, "If you hadn't wasted all that time getting a tour of Ireland, we might have gotten further. We came to get a description of the perp, not to hear her itinerary."

"We'll never get anything out of her if we send her into a catatonic state."

"You do realize, great wannabe social worker, that the more time that goes by the less chance we have of catching the perp."

"Yes, junior officer, I do."

He would have arrested her, if he could have. As it was his anger billowed up into a red face, throbbing veins exposed in his neck. They drove their separate cars back to *The Haven* to report to Mark.

Not surprisingly, when Ravinski told his version of their spat, he left out his opening jab, starting with "Can you imagine what that side-kick of yours called me? A junior officer!"

Gwen was sorry she'd let her temper fly. It wouldn't help their future relationship, and perhaps she'd be shut out of the interview process with Barbara.

Later, when she talked to Mark about it, he said, "I'll see what I can do to mend the riff. I want you to stay on the case."

She knew he, too, was disappointed that she'd let her temper loose.

After hearing Gwen's side, which related both of their invectives, Mark approached the detective.

"It seems you omitted your opening insult."

Ravinski dismissed this.

"If you hope to go back there, Miss Harris will be going with you, and if there's any more abuse, I'll ask the doctor not to allow you back in the patient's room."

Again, Ravinski colored. He turned on his heel and left.

~~~

The search for both suspects continued. Although Sonny was the apparent person responsible, there was no evidence that would eliminate the boyfriend as a suspect.

Sonny was wanted for not reporting to his parole officer. Police and sheriff officers throughout the state were on the lookout for him. So far, only dead ends.

The boyfriend was another matter, since no one seemed to know his real name. Nor did anyone know anything about him— where he hung out, or where he worked, if he did. Backtracking through *The Haven*'s sign-in book, a few names were gathered, but as the record didn't reveal who they were going to visit, this was of little value.

Megan was questioned, because as Charlene's neighbor, she had seen him.

"You're sure you never caught his name?" Ravinski pressed.

"No. As I said, I was never introduced to him."

"And your neighbor never mentioned him."

"No. She didn't talk about this part of her life."

"How did you know he existed?"

Megan breathed a sigh of exasperation. "I saw him a few times, as he was coming down the hall and entering her apartment."

"Did you hear sounds coming from that apartment?"

"What kind of sounds?"

The detective pursed his lips. "Some kind of sadistic play, perhaps."

"Such as?" Megan was turning the tables, making Ravinski squirm.

The detective colored, lit a cigarette. "Whipping sounds, perhaps screams."

"There could have been sounds like that. Not screams, but moaning.

"How often did he come?"

"It varied. Sometimes he appeared to be there a couple times in one week. Then he didn't come for a few weeks. At least, I didn't hear anything."

"I see."

But of course, Detective Ravinski didn't see at all. He was no further ahead than before, and his boss was getting angry. "Two suspects? And you haven't located either one?"

The press wanted resolution in such cases, and didn't take kindly when none was forthcoming. The case was getting cold.

As food from the trays was missing again, it made Mark and Gwen believe that Sonny was still there. But why? Charlene was dead, and that had been his objective. Why would he still be hanging around?

~~~

To add to his troubles, Mark was informed that water was leaking through the ceiling into a second-floor apartment. He'd had his maintenance man check the apartment above, but there was nothing amiss there.

Gwen asked Mark for a master key. "Let me look around, please. Maybe I can find the source."

"I hate to doubt you, but if maintenance can't find it— "

"Will you let me try?"

Mark hesitated. "If it was coming from an apartment that people are living in, they'd have reported it. Let me check with Marketing on any recent vacancies."

"Or where the residents are on vacation."

"Right."

Mark checked. No vacancies.

He checked with the front desk. "No one on that floor on vacation, sir."

"Good idea, though," he said to Gwen. "Not everyone remembers to tell us when they're going away."

She decided to go up there anyway. She began knocking on doors. Some people were out. To those who opened their doors she asked if they had had any plumbing problems. None had. She was especially interested in the apartments that were adjacent to the one that was directly above the one whose ceiling was caving in. But no one answered the door at either of these. She would try again later.

~~~

A new resident appeared in the dining room one evening. There was quite a twitter among the girls, as this man had arrived alone, and besides he stood up straight, had no need of a walker, and was handsome. After dinner, this gentleman sat by the fireplace, and some of the girls joined him and engaged him in conversation.

Peggy Sue introduced herself and the others.

"And may we know your name?" Paula said.

"Mik McLaughlin."

"Oh, an Irishman, am I right?" Peggy Sue all but shouted.

"Of Irish descent, yes. I was born in this country."

"One of us is also Irish," Ruth said coyly. "Can you guess who?"

Before he could reply, Paula asked, "Will you be staying here permanently?"

"I expect so, if by that you meanwhile I'm still alive."

There was a tinkle of laughter.

"Will your wife be joining you?"

"I have no wife. I'm a widower."

Inwardly Megan groaned. They were shameless.

"How sad," Gertrude said.

"You must be very lonely."

"Not at all, I assure you."

Megan stayed a few minutes longer, and then left. There were so few men in the building, that when a single man arrived, it was cause for jubilation, and some of the women became 'groupies'.

The next day Megan was reading in the library, when the new resident sat down opposite her at the large table.

She looked up and he smiled.

"Are you the Irish lady?"

"I am, yes."

"I thought you might be. My parents came from County Claire. May I ask what part of Ireland you, or your ancestors hail from?"

"From Galway, though I've never been to any part of Ireland. Have you?"

"Once. But that was long ago."

They continued to chat until someone else came into the room, and they all settled down to read.

CHAPTER 24

I read about the death of Charlene in the paper. I wondered what would become of all her money. She told me she didn't have any relatives. She probably had stocks and a heavy bank account. I started thinking how it would be a shame to let it all go to waste. Probably it would go to the state or something. I'd sure like to get a piece of it. I wonder if she left a will.

I couldn't stop thinking about it— the will. Maybe I could fake one. I'd need to forge her signature. Then I remembered the poem she'd written for me. I still have it, all hand-written. She even signed it— first name, anyway.

I know the police are looking for me. But if I come forward with the will she gave me a copy of, maybe I can make my claim, and hell, make my movie after all!

I got the poem out and studied her handwriting. I studied it a lot, and practiced writing like she did. I noticed things— like how she made letters like 'g' and 'p' with long tails, and how her capital letters were always real big, like at the beginning of a sentence.

I didn't want to involve a lawyer, so I made up the will myself. Not too shabby, if I do say so myself. Then I got this bartender I know, Maxine, to type it up for me. It looks real official. Now comes the signing. My hands were all sweaty, so I practiced on a blank sheet of paper, until I stopped shaking. Hey, it looks pretty good. I figured it had to be witnessed, so I took it back to the bartender and asked her to do it.

She flatly refused. "I don't want nothin' more to do with that!"

"That's the way you want it?"

"You're damn right."

She was so stubborn about it, I had to forge her name.

I sat on it a while, figuring how I was going to play my cards. I tried to think how Charlene would work it. Should I give it to the police? Or take it to court? Or maybe I'd have to see a lawyer after all.

In my mind I played out these different ways, like we were acting out our stories in her bed, taking Charlene's part too, you know, going back and forth like we used to. In the end, I decided to take it to the police. And by coming in on my own, it might help to establish my innocence.

I went down to the local station, identified myself, said how sorry I was to read in the paper that Miss Osmund had died. I said I was a distant relative of hers, and since she had no other family, she'd left her inheritance to me. She'd given me a copy of her will before she died. I showed it to this Officer Schmaltski. He had me sit down in a little office, and said he'd be back in a minute, taking the will with him. He was gone quite a while and I was getting nervous.

Maybe it was a big mistake, coming forward.

Finally, a detective came into the room with Schmaltski and they sat down. This guy, Detective Bernard started asking me a lot of questions— how long since I'd seen her, what sort of relations were we, what was the nature of our relationship. I didn't see the point to any of this. When I tried to ask a question, like what was the procedure for making the claim, they ignored me, and kept asking me more questions, even the same ones as before.

~~~

Megan's phone rang.

Mark said, "Miss Denison, I had a call from the Police. They have someone there who might be the victim's boyfriend."

"Oh, my. I'm so glad to hear that."

"You would recognize the man, right?"

"Yes, I believe so."

"This is asking a lot, but would you be willing to go to the police station and identify him?"

"Oh, I don't know, Mr. Cranson."

"I could drive you there, and you'd be viewing him from behind a one-way window."

"Can I think about this for a while?"

"Well, the situation now is that he came in on his own free will, claiming he'd been the sole heir to her estate. The police suspect he's the boyfriend, and are stalling, waiting for someone to come in and identify him."

~~~

Detective Bernard told Peter Schoenstein, for that was Brutus's real name, that they were waiting for a handwriting expert to come and compare the writing of this will with known handwriting.

"I can supply that," Peter said. He produced the poem. "She wrote this a while back."

The contents of the poem embarrassed the detective. He tossed it aside.

"Someone is on their way to compare them," he was told. "Let's step into this other room."

Peter was led down the hall to another office. There were three other men in the room, police staff in street clothes.

Peter turned. "What's going on?"

"Just wait here."

~~~

Mark drove up to the police station with Megan and an application form that Charlene Osmund filled out before she moved into *The Haven*. That would establish her handwriting.

"I'm not sure I'm up to this, Mr. Cranson."

"I'll be with you every step of the way."

They were met by Detective Bernard and given instructions.

"There are four men in there. Be very careful. Don't make any hasty judgments. Take your time. If you're not sure, just say so."

"Will he be able to see us?"

"No."

"Or hear us?"

"No. But we won't be talking loudly."

Megan took a deep breath. "OK."

Mark took her arm, and they followed Bernard down the hall to a small room. As soon as she entered she covered her mouth to suppress a cry.

"It's him!"

"Which one?"

"In the black jacket."

"Are you sure? Take a good look."

"It is. I'm positive."

The detective waited.

"We can't make any mistakes here."

"There's no doubt. No doubt at all. I saw him come and go several times to her apartment."

"You mean Miss Osmund's."

"Yes."

Detective Bernard went back into the room with the lineup. He dismissed the other three, and spoke to Peter.

"We're holding you overnight. You're a suspect in the murder of Charlene Osmund."

"Why? I didn't do it."

"We need to make sure of that."

"You can't hold me without charging me."

"We can hold you for twenty-four hours, and then with probable cause, we can charge you."

"Shit!"

A uniformed officer led him down the hall.

"I want a lawyer."

A court-appointed lawyer was sent for.

No further questioning of Peter Schoenstein was made until the court-appointed lawyer assigned to Peter showed up. When he appeared, he was introduced to Peter, and Detective Bernard continued questioning Peter.

"You were a friend of Miss Osmund, right?"

"No, like I said, a distant relative."

"When did you last see her?"

"Oh, gee, it's been a couple of years."

"You live in town here, right?"

"Right."

"But never went to see her."

"She was a lot older than me. I hardly knew her."

"Did you have a financial interest in Miss Osmund?"

"What do you mean?"

"Miss Osmund was wealthy, right?"

"I guess so."

"Did you have an interest in her money?"

"No. How would I know she had a lot of money?"

"You must have noticed her rich surroundings— when you visited her."

"I didn't pay attention. I never expected to inherit any-thing."

"Did you ever discuss money?"

"No. Look, I was real surprised she put me in her will. You could have knocked me over. But hey, she had no one else, you know what I mean?"

"We need you to give us the name of two people who can verify your character."

"Why?"

A paper was shoved across the desk. "Write their names on this paper."

Brutus started to sweat. He turned to his lawyer, who made no objection. God, who should he put? He didn't want to involve anyone at work. The only other contacts he had were guys he'd met at the bar of the Flatiron. He didn't know them that well, but he was pretty sure they'd stand up for him.

He wrote two names down, and pushed the paper back to Bernard. Bernard pushed it back. "Write down their addresses."

"I don't know where they live, but I know where you can find them."

"Where?"

"The Flatiron Bar."

"Write it down."

He did.

"That's all for now."

"Can I go?"

"No. We're holding you overnight."

~~~

Gwen was in Mark's office when Ravinski strode in.

He looked annoyed that she was there, but said nothing.

"We've got the boyfriend in custody."

"Wow, how did that happen?" Mark said.

"He came in on his own. Brought a will he said the deceased had given him a copy of. Obvious forgery. We asked him to give us two character witnesses, and he gave the names of two people who frequent the same bar he does. We're going to need someone undercover to go to that bar and do some digging."

"Are you asking me to go?" Mark said.

Ravinski hesitated, coughed. "Just a thought. I know you want this case solved."

"Gwen piped up. "Let me go."

"No!" rejoined Mark.

Gwen said, "If a strange man tries to talk to those guys they're not likely to open up. But a woman might get them to talk, if she's friendly."

"It's too dangerous," Mark said.

"She's got a point," Ravinski said, "about a woman being more likely to get their attention."

Gwen was getting into it. "I could— what do they call it? Belly up to the bar, and get chatty."

Mark groaned.

"That would work," Ravinski was being unusually pleasant. "We can only hold him overnight without charging him. We don't have enough to go on without further evidence. It's a wild shot."

"What do you hope to find out from these guys?" Mark asked.

"Anything would be helpful. If she could come on to one of them, he'd be more likely to loosen his tongue."

"Hey, wait a minute. She's my girl, she's been through hell, and I don't want to put her at any more risk!"

"Figured that. How about you come in alone, before she does, sit at a table in the back, and make sure nothing funny happens."

"I don't need a chaperone!" Gwen said.

"Yes, you do," Mark said.

Mark took a deep breath, and turned to the detective. "How do you expect her to find out anything significant in one sitting?"

"Don't know. It's an off chance."

Ravinski waited.

Then Mark put his hand on Gwen's. "You don't have to do this. You've already been through so much."

Gwen wasn't waiting for Mark's permission. She said, "I think I'd better costume up."

"Costume up?"

"You know— dress the part."

~~~

At ten minutes to eight, Mark, in jeans and a plaid shirt, entered the Flatiron, sat at a table with a paperback book, ordered and paid for a beer.

Fifteen minutes later, Gwen entered, sauntered up to the bar, and sat down between two men.

Jesus, Mark thought to himself. Dress the part! She wore net stockings, a very short skirt, and a low cut blouse. She had on lots of makeup, and she was wearing a sexy look-alike Marilyn Monroe blonde wig. He had to restrain himself from jumping up and pulling her out of there.

Hell, he thought, I didn't ask you to look like a prostitute, just a girl who comes in for a drink.

"What's your poison?" One of them asked.

She flashed a big smile. "I like white wine."

Both men bought her a drink. She introduced herself as Becky. When they asked, she said she worked at Macy's.

One of them said his name was Bud, and the other, Larry. She remembered the names Brutus had given Ravinski. These men had different names. Finally, she got around to asking, if either of them knew a Peter.

The one called Larry said, "You mean Peter Schoenstein?"

She nodded.

"Sure, I know Peter."

"Does he come here often?

"He should be here tonight. Why?"

She giggled. "Somebody said I should meet him."

"Hey, you've got us. What do you need with him?"

They were taking her off track.

"Well," she tried to sound mysterious, "a friend said we might have something in common."

She didn't know how long she could run this line without coming up with something concrete, but for now she'd just play it by ear.

"Yeah? Like what?"

"That's my secret. What can you tell me about him?"

"He's got one thing on his mind," Larry said. "He's fixated on making this movie. That's all he wants to talk about."

They'd fallen into her lap.

She breathed a sigh of relief; now she had a path. She'd make it up as she went along.

"See, that's what I heard. OK, I'll tell you. I'm an actress. Not a professional, but I've done a lot of community theater. A friend told me this guy was making a movie. And I, well, I wanted to meet him. See if he'd let me try out."

"Yeah? Maybe he'll give us all a part," Larry laughed.

Bud said, "If you'll listen, he'll talk."

"Do you think he's serious about it?" Gwen asked.

"He is if he can find somebody to back him. He was seeing this rich lady, thought he had it in the bag, and then she backed out."

"If you can put up the money, I'm sure he'll give you a part." Larry looked her up and down. "Maybe even if you can't, he'd give a cute little number like you a role," he said, putting his arm around her.

Mark was alert. He wanted to jump up and punch the guy, but he controlled the impulse.

"Hey, Maxine, bring the lady another drink."

"No, no. I haven't finished these."

"What about this rich lady?" Gwen asked. "Why did she back out?"

"Who knows?"

"How did Peter take it?" Gwen asked.

"He was pissed. Thought she betrayed him," Bud said.

"He started a fight in here one night, over nothin," Larry added.

"Yeah, he changed from being higher than a kite to real sour."

The lady tending bar was listening. She stood close to them, drying glasses with a ragged towel. Then she left the bar for a few minutes.

They chatted some more, but Gwen thought her fishing expedition had been successful and wanted to leave.

"Well, I gotta get home," she said. "Looks like your friend isn't showing up tonight. Maybe another time. Thanks for the drinks."

"Oh, Honey, don't leave us. We're just getting warmed up."

"Gotta go. Hubby, you know?"

Their ardor cooled.

"OK, come by again."

She slipped off the stool.

Maxine put a note in her hand. "Here's how you can reach him, if you want to."

"Thanks," she said to Maxine and walked to the door.

Mark watched the men. After they'd watched her leave, they turned back to their drinks and started watching the baseball game on TV. A few minutes later Mark left the bar.

Gwen drove home, and soon after, Mark came in the door.

"Jeez, you love it, don't you?"

"Love what?"

"Flirting with those guys."

"I was just playing the part."

"Over doing it, weren't you? Where'd you get that blonde wig?"

"I got it for a Halloween party years ago. What's gotten into you? I didn't do anything out of line."

"Yeah, I know. What did you find out?"

"I don't know if I want to tell you now."

"Oh, come on. I'm sorry." He waited. "Can I fix you a drink?"

"No, I've had two."

"Right."

She gave him a brief rundown of what she'd learned.

"You may have hit the jackpot."

"How so?"

"Now the police will have something to drill him about."

"That won't prove if he's guilty or not."

"It's a step."

CHAPTER 25

Gwen relayed the information she'd gained at the bar to Ravinski, who in turn reported to Detective Bernard.

"They didn't mention Miss Osmund by name, but they said he talked about having a deal with a rich lady, and how she'd backed out. They said that made Peter very angry."

The next day Detective Bernard met with Peter again.

"We understand you and Miss Osmund were planning a project."

"What project?"

"Did you ever discuss a project you wanted her to support?"

"Like what?"

"Like making a movie."

"There weren't no project."

"I think you better come clean about this or we won't be able to believe anything you say."

Peter broke into a sweat. He knew it was visible. Damn, his buddies at the bar had told the police everything. He felt stupid for having given those names and the name of the bar.

"Ok," he finally said. "We did discuss the movie."

"You were seeing her."

Peter shuffled his feet. "Mostly talked on the phone."

"Go on."

For a while she sounded real interested— we were going to write it together. Then she cooled off."

"And she was going to put up the money?"

"She offered to. I didn't ask her to."

"How would you get the money if she didn't back your project?"

"We didn't discuss that. Like I said, she offered."

"Why did she cool off about it?"

"I don't know. Except maybe . . ."

"Maybe what?"

"She said she had a sister who was very ill. She said she had to do something to help her— get her to this cancer clinic. It's real expensive."

"What's the name of this clinic?"

"I don't know."

"You said she had no other relatives."

Peter coughed. "Sometimes she lied. I never knew when to believe her."

~~~

Around three o'clock on the next day, Gwen remembered the note the bartender had given her. She'd shoved it in her pocket and forgotten about it, perhaps because she knew where this Peter was— in jail. Now she was curious, and got up to read the note.

To her surprise, it wasn't about where to find him at all. It said, "If you want to get the real dirt on Peter, meet me at Manuel's tomorrow at three-thirty." It was signed Maxine.

She looked at her watch. If she hurried, she could make it. She drove as fast as she dared up the highway, into San Rafael and over to Manuel's.

Looking around she saw no Maxine. She sat down in a booth and waited. She'd come in five minutes late; maybe she'd missed Maxine.

She sat wondering what the woman meant by 'dirt'. Was there more to the story than what she'd been told by the guys the night before?

Finally, at three-forty-five, Maxine arrived. In daylight she looked older than she had the night before. She was breathing hard, from running.

No longer a blonde, Gwen knew the woman didn't recognize her. She rose to greet her.

Maxine looked at her in disbelief. "Are you really the girl from the bar last night?"

Gwen nodded. "Yes, I am, Maxine."

"Sorry to be late." She looked around to make sure they wouldn't be heard.

"Just glad you've come." She extended her hand. "I'm Gwen."

Maxine stared at her. "You sure look different."

Gwen smiled. "This is the real me."

Maxine nodded, and they sat down. "I'll probably get in trouble for telling you this. But if Pete had anything to do with that murder, I want him to pay."

"You know about the murder?"

"Sure, it was in the paper. Correct me if I'm wrong, but you were at the bar to find out about Peter. Am I right? Are you with the police?"

"No! Whatever made you think that?"

"Just the way you were acting. Stalling, you know, like you had this secret, but you didn't know what it was."

Gwen wasn't eager to admit her undercover role. "Tell me what you know," she said.

"OK. He drew up some sort of homemade will, in handwriting, and brought it to me to type up. I shouldn't have, I know. But I did. Then he planned to forge— "

A waiter came to take their order, and they both asked for coffee. After he left Maxine looked sort of blank.

"Where was I?"

"You were saying something about forgery."

"Oh, yeah. When he brought the will back, he 'd already forged that lady's name, and now he wanted me to witness it for him. I said 'No', and he said he'd pay me, fifty dollars. I still refused, and he got mad. Then, when I got off work that night, he was waiting for me outside in the dark. When I refused, he slapped me up. Then he took off."

Gwen said, "Go on."

"I know that's a fake will and that rich lady never left him a dime."

Gwen kept wondering why the woman was telling her all this.

"He's really a scumbag," Maxine said.

"You've known him a long time?"

"Yeah. Me and him used to be a number. Then he just dropped me like a hot potato. But he kept coming in the bar, talking up other girls, right in my face."

Now Gwen understood. This was revenge.

"You're a nice lady, and I wouldn't have anything to do with him, if I were you. Not even if he did give you a part in a movie."

"Are you willing to tell this to the police— how you typed up the false will?"

Maxine squirmed. Then she said, "Couldn't you just tell them somebody told you this?"

"No, it wouldn't hold up. Did you use your real name, Maxine?"

"Yeah. That was dumb, huh?"

"Will you come to the police station with me?"

Maxine hesitated. "I've got to be at work at five."

"We have time. I'll drive you."

"Will I get in trouble?"

"I can't say for sure. But the fact that you're giving them so much information, and confessing your part in this scheme will probably mitigate any charges against you."

Maxine finally agreed to accompany Gwen to the police station.

They met with Ravinski. Gwen spoke to him first, stating that this woman had come forth on her own and told her story. She urged Ravinski to go easy on her.

Ravinski was so pleased to be getting at the root of Peter's motives that he simply asked her to write down her story and sign it. Nothing was said about her typing up the false document.

~~~

The source of the leak in the ceiling still had not been identified. Gwen was determined to find it. She couldn't help wondering if it had something to do with Sonny, but she couldn't figure out the connection he'd have with the leaking water. If he were hiding in an apartment, he'd be careful not to call attention to himself.

She didn't want to ask Mark for the key again, but while waiting for him in his office, she looked in his drawers and found a master key to all apartments. She felt a little guilty, but at least this way she'd be responsible, not involving Mark.

She went back to the third floor. Knocking on the doors adjacent to the one above the leaky unit, but again she got no response at either. She used the key to enter one, called out, no one answered. She poked her head in the bedroom and bathroom; no one was there.

She did the same at the other apartment. Still no one answered, but there were some clothes in the bedroom. She noticed the bathroom door was locked— the occupant was in there! She felt like an intruder and got out of there quickly.

~~~

The next evening when Gwen knocked on her aunt's door, there was no response. She let herself in with her own key. Megan was not there. Fear caused her heart to start racing, as she could only conceive of the worst circumstances. She found the other girls going to dinner, and asked if they'd seen her aunt. No one had.

"Do you know where she could be?" Gwen asked.

"No. She usually joins us for dinner. We waited for her," Peggy Sue said.

"Maybe she's in the exercise room," Marjorie said.

Arlene said, "Or on the bus."

The girls were concerned too. Gwen checked the community rooms, but could not find her. She contacted Mark. He had no information, either.

"I think she would have told me if she were going out," said Gwen.

"Did she expect you this evening?" Mark asked.

"No, not specifically. But I often drop by, as you know, and with an unsolved murder, we keep in touch pretty regularly."

Mark nodded.

"I'll wait in her room, until she comes back, if she's gone out."

"Would you like me to wait with you?"

Gwen smiled at him. "Yes, I would."

They walked back to Megan's apartment and let themselves in.

~~~

I can't believe I'm stuck in this tub for two days, and can't get out. The knob came apart, with the screw part on the other side. I pushed my hands against the glass and tried to slide it open. I've tried and tried. It won't budge. If there were a shower in this tub, I could break the glass with the shower head, but no, this tub doesn't have a shower!

That librarian sure tricked me. Imagine— I go into the room of this Charlene, smother her, and guess what? It's not my fuckin' sister after all! Even in the dark I could tell. I killed the wrong woman! I still don't have my Charlene. Damn! I have to get out of this joint, but I've got unfinished business.

~~~

At nine o'clock, Gwen heard a key in the lock, and Megan let herself in.

"Where have you been?" Gwen cried in relief.

Megan looked puzzled. "Is something wrong?"

"No, we were just worried. You weren't here. Your friends didn't know where you were."

"I went out."

"Oh."

Silence.

"I didn't know I had to report to you, Gwen."

"Well, no, of course not. It's just that, well— "

"That I never do, is that it?"

"I guess I thought you'd tell me. And with the killer still possibly on the premises."

"Gwen, you've been very kind, with all your concern for me, but really, I'm a grown woman and I can take care of myself. You needn't hover, dear."

"I'm sorry," Gwen rose to go, as did Mark.

They walked together down the hall.

"She made me feel like I was snooping."

"Perhaps she feels her privacy is being invaded."

"I suppose. What should I do— ignore her?"

"No, but guess our waiting up for her like worried parents was the wrong move."

"Right. Wonder where she went. She wasn't about to tell us."

"No. Her secret, for now anyway."

After kissing passionately for fifteen minutes in his office, Gwen said she had to leave. Mark walked her to her car, and they said good-night.

CHAPTER 26

When she got home and picked up her mail, there was an officious looking letter from the court. A date for her trial was set for a week away, again at nine o'clock. It was signed by the lawyer who said he was representing her. Again, it was a different attorney. She wanted to discuss the case with him. In the morning she called and left a message. By now she wasn't surprised that she got no response. In late afternoon she decided to go to the defenders' office, and try to see him directly. She left work in time to make it to the office before they closed.

Surprise, surprise. The lawyer was in and asked her into a tiny cubicle, which appeared to be one used by any defender interviewing a client.

"I'd like to know if you've read the letter I wrote some time ago to the expeditor," she began.

"Which expeditor? We have many."

"I don't know. I was just told to address my letter to 'the expeditor'."

The lawyer, a Mr. Conway, looked through her file. "I don't see it here. No, I don't have it."

Gwen's shoulders slumped.

"Do you know where my letter might be?"

Mr. Conway shook his head.

"I have a carbon at home. Shall I bring it in?"

He shrugged. "If you like. I'm not sure it will be relevant."

"I was requesting that the case be dropped, as it wasn't hit and run at all."

"It's too late for that. It has to go to trial now."

"Do you have the police report in that file? I was told I could only get it from you."

"Yes." He handed it to her.

She skimmed through it, caught phrases like "significant damage", "refused to co-operate." She could hardly contain herself. How could he? So untrue.

She tried to remember the gist of what was in her letter.

"Although I didn't think I'd caused the scratch on his car, I offered to pay, in cash. At this point, he yelled that I was trying to evade the law by not giving him my insurance information, and said he would report it to the police."

"If you didn't think you'd caused the accident, why did you offer to pay?"

Gwen felt trapped. "He frightened me. He seemed out of control."

"I doubt that a jury would find you innocent."

"Why?"

"People seldom offer to pay for damage they didn't cause."

He let that sink in.

"But I'll do what I can to defend you."

It was surreal. Gwen couldn't even remember going to her car and driving to *The Haven*. How could this trivial matter have escalated to this extent?

She sat in her old VW, taking a few deep breaths, and remembering what it was she wanted to do at *The Haven*. As it came back to her, the experience at the courthouse faded into the background, at least for the moment.

Something had been bothering her about the room with the clothes. She hadn't been able to get in the bathroom because it was locked. Surely it wouldn't be now, and she could check for the leak.

When she reached *The Haven*, the woman at the desk informed her that her aunt would like to see her.

"I'm sorry, Gwen, about last night. I will tell you why I was out. I didn't want the director to know my private business."

"I understand."

"There's a new resident here. He took me out to dinner."

"Really? That's great."

"Well, it's just for company you understand, but he is very nice."

"What's his name?"

"Michael, or Mik McLaughlin."

"Ah, an Irishman."

"Yes, I asked him if he invited me out because I was Irish, and he said no, that he found me more interesting and more attractive than the others." She giggled in embarrassment.

"You are interesting. And you're definitely attractive, Megan. You could have another whole life."

"Oh, go on now. I'm fifty-one."

"The other girls, as you call each other, are much older— some in their eighties."

"There are two that I know of in their nineties."

"Well, there you are— twice your age. I'm happy for you."

Megan giggled again. "Being Irish, you know, I asked him if he was a practicing Catholic, and he said, 'I'm well past practicing, Love.'"

Gwen smiled. "I'm happy for you, Megan."

"Don't tell Mark or anyone else. I can do without the talk. You wouldn't believe the gossip in this place. If you seek grief counseling everyone knows it. If you have a root canal everyone knows it."

"Mum's the word."

"And don't make too much of this, Gwen— it was just a date. I may never see him again."

"But you like him, I can tell. What is it about him that appeals to you?"

"Besides his being a nice man and a good listener? Well, he stands up straight."

Gwen laughed. Yes, that would definitely be in a man's favor.

Just then the lights went out. Gwen checked in the hall, lights out there too.

"It's probably a power outage. It's the second time this week."

"What's going on?"

"Who knows?"

"I'd better get going. Do you keep a flashlight for such occasions?"

"Yes, I have two."

As it was summer, there was still a bit of light coming from the outside which provided some illumination in the room.

Megan made her way to a kitchen drawer. "Here's one for you."

Gwen accepted it, and kissed Megan good-bye.

"Be careful now, on the stairs. You know the elevator won't be working."

"I will."

Gwen walked down one flight of stairs, and then along the darkened hall of the third floor.

She reached the room she wanted, and knocked on the door. When no one answered she let herself in with the key she had purloined.

"Anyone home?" she called.

She placed her purse on the table by the door, and entered the bedroom. With the flashlight on, she could see the same clothes on the bed that had been there before; they were men's. She headed toward the bathroom, which had been locked the day before. It still was, which alarmed her. With her hairpin she managed to pick it open. Although she could hear no running water, the bathtub had overflowed and water on the floor was half an inch deep.

It was contained behind the marble ledge separating the bath from the rest of the apartment. Someone appeared to be in the tub, but the glass was not transparent, she couldn't see who it was.

"Who's in there?" she called. "Are you OK?"

When no one answered, she was concerned that the occupant may have passed out, had a stroke, or even died in the tub. She reached for the knob to open the glass, but it was missing. Seeing part of it on the floor she picked it up; the screw which attached the two parts together was in the knob she held.

She knocked on the glass. "Can you hear me?"

No response. Afraid the person inside was in real danger, she used the attached towel bar to push the door aside. Before it was all the way open, a hand reached out and grabbed her.

"Welcome to my hideout," he said, pulling her toward him.

She jerked away as hard as she could, but Sonny yanked her until she fell forward landing with a big splash on her hands and knees into the water-filled tub.

Spluttering and spitting, she managed to turn and sit up.

"You're just the person I need," he cried. "You and that librarian tricked me. That wasn't my sister at all. I killed the wrong fuckin' person!"

Gwen was practically catatonic. She couldn't speak, as this naked man stood above her, again threatening her.

"I've been locked in here for two days. Now I'm getting out. But you're staying here 'til I get dressed."

He got out of the tub, and using the attached towel bar, shut the glass door. "Now see how you like it."

She could hear him toweling off, and heading for the bedroom. She placed her hands against the glass and pushed. Nothing happened. It wouldn't budge. Why, she wondered. She could slide it from the outside.

She still had the knob with the screw in her hand. Perhaps she could push the screw into the hole in the glass to open the door. Gently, she tried it out; she could do it. But now what? Her heart was throbbing, as she tried to stay calm and think if there were any way to escape. The only possibility, she decided, was to dash for the door before he was dressed. He wouldn't want to chase her down the hall half-naked, would he?

Heavy with wet clothes, she opened the glass door, ran out of the bathroom and toward the door to that hallway. Just as she reached the door, he grabbed her, she screamed, he pulled her back, and threw her to the floor.

"You didn't seriously think you could get away, did you?"

"What is it you want, Sonny?" she said struggling to her feet.

"I want to find my sister, and you're going to help me."

"You, you did find her."

"No. You knew that, didn't you? That wasn't my sister!"

"I didn't know that."

"We're going to your house."

"What!"

"You're going to make some calls. We're going to find out where my goddamned sister is. We'll just wait a little longer, until these old folks bed down for the night, and then we're leaving."

Gwen couldn't believe it was happening again.

She tried to hedge. "My roommate might be there."

"She got married, remember?"

Had she told him that?

It was a warm evening, but in her wet clothes Gwen began to shiver. Perhaps it was fear. Or shock.

Sonny finished buttoning his shirt. He walked to the bedroom, yanked a blanket off the bed, returned and tossed it to Gwen.

"Put this around you."

She did. For a moment she remembered the tender side of this man. But no, she mustn't forget that he was violent, dangerous, and she mustn't let her guard down.

"We'll give it another hour or so," he said.

They sat in silence in the dark, while Sonny bit off his fingernails, spitting them out in predictable intervals.

Gwen tried to think of where and how she'd escape. No doubt he'd force her down the back stairs, so there'd be no help from the front desk. Her only chance was running into someone in the hall, who hopefully would see her dilemma, and call for help.

Where was Mark now that she needed him? And where exactly in the bathroom was her flashlight?

The moon rose in the east, casting its light into the room.

Suddenly, Sonny started to talk.

"You wanna hear the story, how I got in this mess?"

"All she wanted was to escape, but she said,"Yes."

"OK. My sister and I were on a run out to West Marin to pick up another drop from Canada. Can't you go any faster?" I said.

"Not on this bumpy road," she said.

It was 1932— Prohibition, and we're boot-leggers. We're heading out just north of Pt. Reyes, on a lonely cutoff road to make our pickup on the beach.

Charlene had just had super stiff suspensions installed to keep the car from sagging under the enormous weight of a full load, but it was still a bumpy ride.

"The boat's probably there already, and they won't hang around waiting for us. Not with that cargo," I said.

"Just shut up, Sonny. It's just as dangerous to be there too early— sitting duck for the feds."

"I know, I know." I started chewing my fingernails.

We drove in silence for another five minutes, and then Charlene said, "I'm going to turn the lights out now."

Not even a moon. But we always cut our lights as we approached our target. Too dangerous to drive with head-lights— federal agents or cops could be parked out there, just waiting for the likes of us.

There wasn't even a road now, just field grass we were bumping across. Finally, Sis came to a stop.

"I think we're safe here," she said. "You see anything out there?"

I peered around in my seat. "No. Do you?"

"No, but they're not going to send up flares either. Walk down to the beach and see if you can see anything."

I did. It was pitch dark, and a fog coming in. I couldn't see a damn thing. And quiet— couldn't hear the waves, wind— nothing. Just the lonely sound of a seagull off shore some place. I waited. It wasn't that cold, but I was shivering. I had a bad feeling about this run. We'd done it many times before, but something didn't seem right to-night. I couldn't put my finger on it.

I waited, standing up. Then I waited sitting down, but my pants were getting wet from the damp sand, and made me colder. I stood up and walked along the shore in the direction the boat would be coming from— north, from Canada.

After waiting about half an hour, just coming around a bend, I could just make out a boat hugging the shore.

As it got closer I ran back to the car.

"They're coming in!"

Charlene flashed her lights twice— one long and one short to signal we were here.

The moon began to peek out behind the clouds, and we could see someone drop anchor. We could just make out two guys, apparently shifting crates into the rowboat they'd lowered into the water. Charlene and me stood outside the car, straining our eyes to see better. Not just the boat, but surrounding area, scanning for any other ac-tivity.

Sometimes another pickup vehicle would come along and we'd get scared, thinking it was the police or the feds, but it was usually just another pickup car. This place made a perfect contact point, because it was real remote, and off the beaten road. Hardly anybody knew about it.

"Go on down to the beach and help them," Charlene said. I don't want to turn the lights on again.

I did. When I got there, they were still off-shore loading the rowboat. I gave a low whistle; they looked up, and soon they were in the small boat, coming toward me. The moon was shining on the water now. It was still so quiet, I could hear the oars move in the water, like they were cutting through liquid moonlight.

The men approached the shore, jumped out, and tried to pull the rowboat up on the beach. It was so heavy with its cargo, even with me giving them a hand, it was hard work.

Then we carried the booze, case by case through the grassy sand up to the car. Nobody said anything. We just made one trip after another, until we had all the cases in the trunk of the Ford.

We were just getting ready to pull away when we heard shouts of "Halt." Charlene turned her flashlight in that direction, and we could see two officers coming toward us.

The boatmen ran for the water.

Charlene yelled, "Get in the car."

We did. She'd left the motor running, so we took off, but the officers were on us, shot out our two back tires, and we stalled in the sand.

"Get out! Get under the car," she said.

While we were running around the car, we heard "Halt!" again. Then a shot. We both got under the car, with our heads looking out.

Charlene pulled out her pistol. The officers came closer. Then another shot. I couldn't tell where it came from-- Charlene's gun, I guess.

Everything after that was total confusion. An officer was down. The other one came at me, and at gunpoint forced me to get out from under the car, and lean over the hood. Where was Charlene? Jesus, did she manage to get away? With his gun pointed at me, he knelt down and listened to his partner's heart, and felt around the artery on the side of the neck.

Then he picked up Charlene's gun, the officer's gun, and stood up hollering "Shit! Shit! Shit!" over and over again.

He pushed me, with my arms behind my head in front of him across the sand for about a quarter of a mile to where the cops' car was.

"Where was Charlene?"

Sonny stopped talking as suddenly as he'd started. He went into a deep reverie as he relived, this the turning point in his life. Tears were running down his face. His whole body reflected the despair and anguish of this incident had cost him. He seemed totally unaware that anyone else was in the room.

Just as suddenly he jerked back into the present and continued his story.

"When we got there, he made me get in the rear. There was a barrier between the front and back seats. Then he drove to where his partner was. He opened the trunk, and made me get out and help him lift the dead cop into the trunk. Then he pushed me back in the car.

We drove back the way we'd come, until we arrived at the police station in the town of Pt. Reyes. All the time I'm wondering what happened to my sister. Soon as he got me in the station, I heard them send another squad car out there to retrieve Charlene's car with all the cargo.

After that, it was just a nightmare. It happened so fast, I couldn't believe it. Without much ado that night I was put in the slammer. I was kicked a couple of times, and somebody shouted, "Killing a cop is a death sentence!"

Who killed the cop? I couldn't think. Charlene must have done it before she ran out on me. I know I didn't. I didn't even know how to shoot.

"What do you think?"

"I'm very sorry all that happened to you."

"Yeah, but who shot the gun?"

"I don't know, but I wouldn't jump the gun, assuming your sister did."

As soon as she'd said that unintentional pun, she bit. her lip.

"Are you saying *I* did?" He rose in anger and came toward her. He had worked himself into a sweat, and warm drops of perspiration fell on her shivering body.

Then he turned and faced the window.

"I'm sorry, Sonny. I didn't mean it that way. Listen, I have to use the bathroom."

He glared at her.

"Please."

They'd played this scene before, so he let her go, stood outside the door and waited for her to return.

She did have to go, but she was also hoping to find the flashlight. Well, there it was, in the tub, light out.

She returned to the living room with Sonny, "I think we can safely get out of here now. Come on."

She was sure he planned to use her car. The thought occurred to her that she might be able to place a fly in the ointment by leaving her purse in the room, which meant she wouldn't have any keys. What would he do then?

The question was moot; he picked up her purse as they made their exit from the room.

Holding her arm tightly, he directed her down the hall, but did not turn toward the stairs. To her surprise, he stopped by the wall at the end of the hall and opened an ordinary looking door which concealed another. He pressed a button, turned a handle, and something half the size of an elevator appeared before her.

"Get in," he said.

"What is this?"

"A dumb waiter."

She balked.

"Get in. It's safe enough. It can hold up to four hundred pounds."

"This is how you've been getting around?"

"Yup. Clever, huh? They had one at Folsom. Course I never got in that one."

He helped, forced her inside. The space was tight, as they shared it with a large metal rack full of empty shelves meant for carrying trays.

The ride down was bumpy. They got off in the garage, his leading her through the dark halls until they were by the entrance.

Gwen watched each opportunity fade away, along with any hope of escaping.

He got her outside, then handed her the purse. "Get the keys out."

Afraid to challenge him, she did so.

"Now where's your car?"

Scanning the lot for any sign of life, someone she could alert, she finally said, "I don't remember."

He jerked her arm. "Yes, you do. Where is it?"

She pointed toward a street light. "Over there, I think."

They walked in that direction, Gwen desperately hoping to see a human, or be spotted by one.

"It's not here, is it? I don't want to get rough with you, but I will if you play any more tricks on me."

She'd procrastinated long enough. One more try at Karate. Maybe this move would keep him down long enough to get away. Again, she broke from him, ran a bit, turned to face him, took him down by kicking him in the balls. Yelling and swearing, he lay writhing in pain.

Gwen ran and scooted behind the cars. She prayed that when he rose, he wouldn't be able to find her. When she thought it safe, and still shielded by a row of vehicles, she moved farther away from him, and closer to the building. Removing her shoes, she walked silently in her bobby sox.

She couldn't hear or see anything. He must still be on the ground. She continued moving along the rows, occasionally changing lanes.

A car entered the parking lot. Gwen ran toward it and tried to flag the driver down. He misunderstood, gave her a friendly wave and moved on.

Suddenly, Sonny clapped his hand over her mouth, turned her around and slapped her in the face. Slapped her so hard she'd have fallen if he hadn't caught her.

"How often you going to try that? You'll never outrun me. You know that. Where's your car?" he spat through his teeth.

Holding her face, which throbbed and made her feel woozy, Gwen allowed him to drag her to it.

He pushed her on the passenger side, and got in the driver's side. "Sausalito. South, right?"

He got to the highway and turned south. When they reached Sausalito, he said, "Now you have to give me directions to your place."

"Keep going down Bridgeway."

If only they'd hit a red light.

"When do I turn off?"

"The other end of town."

"You better not be shittin' me."

Her face was throbbing. She had a headache. Did she dare try another means of escape?

The light ahead was turning yellow. Just as he reached the corner it turned red, but Sonny kept going.

Damn!

There was only one more traffic light in town. Please, God, let it turn red.

"We're lookin' for a house, or what?"

"Yes, it's a house."

The light was red. He stopped. She opened the door and got one foot on the ground. He yanked her back in, reached across and slammed the door shut. Then he twisted her arm until she cried out.

"I warned you. You had that coming."

As the road left the water's edge and turned west, she directed him up the hill to Third Street. He parked, ironically in front of her enemy's car. Too close for comfort.

He held on to her arm as they made their way to her steps and porch.

"Where's the house key?"

"On that same ring."

"You get it open."

He gave her the key ring, and she opened the door. She turned on the living room light.

"Now we're going to work," he said. "Sit down there, by the phone."

"I'd like to get into some dry clothes," she said as firmly as she could.

He looked annoyed, but he let her go to her bedroom.

"I know about escaping through windows, so I'm coming with you. I won't watch or anything. I ain't a prevert."

He followed her into the bedroom, and turned his back, as Gwen scrambled to get into some dry jeans and a sweater.

Of course, I wanted her. I'm normal, you know. Don't think I didn't want to grab that girl, who must be naked by now, and throw her down on the bed and have her. I was getting excited just thinking about it, and imagining what she looked like without any clothes. I'd only had a woman twice— just before I was put in the cooler. Had plenty of the other in prison— even got to like it after a while, but I was always wishing for a woman. Lord, I was frustrated. I really wanted to take her, even with her messed up face.

But I've got my morals, you know what I mean? I couldn't do anything but stand there, until she was dressed.

When she was finished she said, "Now I'm getting some ice for my face." Gwen went to the refrigerator, with Sonny on her heels. She broke up a tray of ice and wrapped it in a towel.

He said, "Now I have to use the can and you're coming with me. Where is it?"

Sonny pushed her into the bathroom and closed the door. She turned her back.

When he finished, she pushed her way to the sink and looked at her face in the mirror. It was a mess.

Sonny endured the time it took her to wash up and dab some kind of ointment on a cut. Then he led her back to the phone.

"Sit down. Call information and see if they have a Charlene Dickens here in Marin. Maybe she didn't change her name at all."

Holding the ice to her face, she dialed '0' for information.

She didn't expect this to lead anywhere and it didn't.

"Now try San Francisco."

She did, and amazed, she was given a number.

"You're serious? They gave you this number?"

She nodded.

"Dial it. Ask for her, and if she comes to the phone, ask her, um . . ." He hadn't planned this far ahead.

"It's after mid-night."

"You think I care? Call her."

Gwen dialed the number. Sonny leaned in to listen. After three rings someone picked up. "Char's Place. Can I help you?"

He nearly jumped out of his skin. "That was what we called her as a kid! Give me the phone."

He jerked it out of Gwen's hand and spoke into the phone, "Is Char there?"

"We're about to close. Is this a member?"

Sonny wet his dry lips. Member of what? He tried to hedge. "I'd like to talk to her about that."

"Would you mind calling back tomorrow?"

"Aw, Miss. I'm only in town for tonight."

"It's after hours, sir."

"Tell her we knew each other in the old days. Tell her my name is Bingo from when we ran rum together. We're old buddies. She'll remember."

"I'll see if she'll come to the phone."

"Naw, don't bother. If you give me the address, I'll come over tomorrow and surprise her."

She hesitated. Then, "It's 2439 Octavia."

He wrote the address down on the back of her grocery list. "Thanks a lot."

He replaced the receiver and turned to Gwen. "Can you beat that? After all this time, and two murders on my head. And here she was all this time, using her own name. That fuckin' librarian tricked me on purpose."

"*Two* murders?"

"Yup. The woman I dumped down the trash chute, and the wrong Charlene."

"The woman you pushed down the trash chute isn't dead, Sonny. She's hanging in there."

"Glad to hear it. But there's still the other one."

"What are you going to do?"

"Go after her, what d'you think?"

"You can't, Sonny. You don't want another murder on your head."

"Got to. What's one more? Anyway, it makes the first two just wasted unless I get my target."

Gwen turned this twisted logic over in her mind, but she supposed it made some sort of sense to him.

"You got any grub here? I'm starving."

Gwen shrugged. "Look in the fridge."

He procured for himself a cold chicken thigh and some coleslaw, then washed down with a quart of milk.

"Mm, good. Thanks, thanks a lot," he said politely when he finished.

He never ceased to amaze her. Maybe manners learned long ago slipped in on auto pilot when he wasn't thinking.

Then he turned to her and said, "I don't know what I'm gonna do with you."

Gwen tried to remain calm as she wondered if he were contemplating murdering her too.

"But for now, you're coming with me, so you can't call the police."

"Now? You're going now?"

"We're going now." He pulled her up from her chair.

Then he turned to her, holding both of her arms gently. "I just want to say something to you before, before this adventure comes to a head." He licked his lips. "I didn't want to hurt you, you understand? You made me. But I like you, I got nothing against you. In fact, I admire your spirit."

He let go of her arms. "I don't blame you for what you did to me. I'd have done the same if I was you."

Embarrassed by this personal confession, he turned quickly. "Let's go."

She was glad to be going. Afraid, but thinking that her only chance to escape would be when he confronted his sister. She picked up her ice pack as they left the house.

This time Sonny got Gwen in the driver's seat, and then as she moved over, got in himself.

"I'm getting smarter, see? Ain't gonna give you a chance to jump while I'm running around the car."

Once again he warned her of dire consequences should she get any ideas.

As they headed across the bridge and into San Francisco, Sonny was quiet.

Finally, he asked, "What kind of place is this? Gotta be a member."

Gwen had an idea, but she kept it to herself.

They crossed the Golden Gate Bridge, with the full moon shining on the Bay.

They drove in silence through the dark, the streets mostly deserted this time of night.

"You got any maps in there?" he said motioning to the glove box.

"I know how to get there."

"You do?"

"It's on Octavia. I think that's just before Franklin."

"Are you sure? Are you puttin' me on?"

"Just keep going on Lombard."

"You better be telling the truth."

He followed her directions and turned right onto Octavia. As they climbed the roller coaster hill they passed block after block of regal Victorian homes, with curved windows, intricate carved 'gingerbread' detail on the exteriors, which were painted a contrasting color, sometimes gold. Several had small conical turrets.

"Can't see the damn house numbers."

Gwen said, "There's one. 2006. Must be on the other side of the street— uneven number."

They went up another three blocks, and Sonny parked the car. "Gotta be near here."

They walked across the street and started looking for house numbers.

A man was approaching them, walking his dog. This was her chance.

She turned to him, "Could you tell me where 2439 is?"

She reached down to pet his dog, at the same time trying to convey a look of desperation to him, without Sonny seeing her.

"I don't know," the man said. "I don't live on this street."

He continued walking with his dog. She called after him.

"Wait!"

He stopped and turned.

She jerked away from Sonny and ran up to him, "Is your dog an Australian sheep dog? I used to have one."

Then she whispered to him, "Help me. I'm being kidnapped."

CHAPTER 27

When Bernard read the statement Maxine had signed, he spoke with Peter again.

"We now possess knowledge that you fabricated a false will, naming you as the sole recipient of Miss Osmund's estate."

Peter stared at him. At last he said, "I don't know what you're talking about."

"I think you do. Would you like me to read Maxine Redman's statement to you?"

"Yeah."

Detective Bernard did so. He looked up at the end and saw Peter sweating again.

"She lied! She's the one falsifying documents. I never went to her. I barely know her."

"I don't believe you."

"That's your problem."

"We believe you wanted Miss Osmund to back your film. When she refused, you killed her. Then to get her money you falsified a will."

"I did no such thing. You have no proof!"

"We have proof that you wrongfully attempted to obtain her estate."

Peter's nose was running. He rubbed it off on his sleeve as he blurted out, "You call a man a criminal because he wants to follow his dream?"

By now he was sobbing.

"Peter Schoenstein, we're going to hold you here for willfully fabricating a false will in your favor, and for suspicion of murdering Charlene Osmund."

"Even if I did make up the will that don't mean I killed her!"

His sobs alternated with loud cries.

The session had given Bernard a lot to go on.

~~~

The man understood Gwen, took her hand and they started to run. It didn't take long for Sonny to catch up with them, swearing as he approached. He yanked hold of Gwen. Just then the dog nipped at Sonny's ankles, causing him to swear some more. The man, perhaps not wanting to have to put the dog down for having bitten someone, pulled his dog away, leaving Gwen with her captor.

"That was stupid," Sonny fumed, practically pulling her arm out of its socket.

He marched her along the sidewalk, looking for house numbers.

"You don't need me anymore," she said. "Please let me go."

"You can call the cops? No way."

They found 2431. Then 2435. "Gotta be the next one," Sonny said.

And there it was— 2439. Still gripping Gwen's arm, Sonny gazed up at it. Whether taken by its stylish glory, the gold glitter on the gingerbread trim, or a reluctance to pursue his plan, Gwen wasn't sure, but Sonny just stood there, staring at the house. There were lights on in some of the upstairs rooms, and what appeared to be the parlor was dimly lit.

Gwen was shivering. San Francisco is seldom warm, even in the summer, and the evenings are downright chilly.

"So this is the lifestyle my sister's had, while I was. . . Not too shabby."

Again, he clamped his hand around her arm. As they climbed the stairs, Gwen's heart beat harder with each step.

Sonny tried to look through the stained-glass on the front door window. But the prism effect made whatever was behind the glass a blur. From inside they could hear soft voices. Gently, Sonny tried the doorknob. It was locked, as he expected. He rubbed his hands together, then knocked on the door. As no one came, he figured he hadn't knocked hard enough. Applying more strength, he knocked again. In a few moments, the porch light went on and the door was opened. A young lady in sexy regalia faced them.

"What can I do for you?"

She seemed surprised to see a woman with the man.

"I want to see Char."

She shook her head. "We're closed. Who shall I tell her is calling?" As it was after midnight, the young woman looked very suspicious.

"Like I told the lady on the phone I'm an old friend, name's Bingo."

"I'll see if she's awake."

The woman left the door slightly ajar, and turned to go. When she was out of sight, Sonny, pulling Gwen along, pushed the door open and entered the foyer.

Within their view, they could see two gentlemen sitting by the fire smoking cigars. With them were two young ladies.

The men glanced over to see who'd come in, but then returned their attention to the ladies and their drinks.

"What kind of place is this?" Sonny whispered.

To Gwen, it was obvious that it was a brothel.

"A whore house?" he mumbled.

She shrugged.

A grand staircase stood before them. This is probably where she'll come down, Gwen thought. Her heart wouldn't stop throbbing, she had trouble breathing, and she thought she might faint. Was she about to witness a murder? How did he intend to do it? She hadn't seen his knife. She was quite sure he wasn't carrying a gun.

Footsteps were heard on the stairs. A rather heavy-set woman was coming down. Gwen watched Sonny watching the woman descend. Was this his sister? Gwen couldn't tell from the expression his face whether there was recognition there or not.

Finally, in the dim light, wearing a Japanese Kimono, the woman stepped off the last stair and placed her feet on the tile floor.

"Bingo?"

"Don't you recognize me?" Sonny asked.

She looked more closely. "No." She took a step closer. "Wait, you're. . ."

"Yes, sister, your long lost brother."

"Sonny," she said, relaying neither joy nor dismay. "Come in."

"I didn't come here for pleasantries," he all but screamed. "I came to even the score. You let me rot in that prison for thirty-five years for something I didn't do! You never even came to see me— "

As he said these words he lunged toward her, got her by the throat and started squeezing.

Gwen wanted to run, but she was mesmerized by what she saw and stood frozen.

The two men who'd been sitting by the fireplace wasted no time rising and coming to Char's rescue. Together they pulled Sonny back, who was dragging Char with him, until one of them managed to loosen Sonny's hands from her neck.

Char was coughing and choking, but she stood her ground in front of Sonny.

"You deserve to die!" Sonny yelled. "I've been waiting thirty-five years to do this." Again he lunged toward her.

But the two men pulled him away before he got her, and pushed him toward the door.

"No," Char called in a hoarse voice. "Bring him over here, and set him down. I want to talk to him."

Char motioned for the girls to leave, and Sonny was pushed in a chair, with the men still holding him down.

"Now you listen to me," Char said.

Sonny pulled against his restraints. "I have to kill you. You understand that?"

One of the men clipped him on the head and told him to shut up.

"Want us to call the police?" the other asked.

"No. You listen, little brother. I didn't want to stop visiting you— "

"Then why did you?" he shrieked.

"When you stop yelling I'll tell you." She took a deep breath and rubbed her neck. "I did visit you in the beginning. I couldn't get it through your head that you had killed the officer."

In spite of the men, he managed to rise from the chair and lunge at her. "I did not kill that officer. You're the only one who could have!"

The men got him back in the chair.

Charlene went on. "You kept yelling at me and saying I did it. It wasn't me, Sonny. It was you."

"You're lying! You're fucking lying." He kicked the chair in front of him.

"It was your fingerprints on the gun, Sonny. I'd had the gun, yes, but you were holding it when it went off. Finally, I gave up, and didn't come to see you anymore. It was useless."

Sonny blinked, started to say something, then didn't.

Char said, "I tossed the gun in your direction. I wasn't holding it when it went off."

"You told me to shoot!"

"Yes, I did. In the panic of the moment, I did."

"And then you cut out of there. You left me to face those cops alone!"

"I'm very sorry about that."

"You abandoned me!" Tears were running down his face. "You fuckin' just left me there alone, Charlene. Of all times, you abandoned me." He was sobbing.

Charlene approached him, but not too closely. "I truly am sorry, Sonny."

He looked up at her, his nose as well as his eyes running. "Sorry's not enough. I spend thirty-five years in prison, and you got off scot free."

"But I didn't kill the cop."

"Why would I shoot? I never hurt anyone."

She sat down, and asked for water. When it came, she drank a little. Then she spoke calmly. "Because, dear brother, you always did what I told you to."

"Always, always did . . .what you told me to." He shook his head. "No, No, I couldn't have."

Always did what I told you to. The words reverberated in his head over and over.

As he stared at his sister. Gwen could see a multitude of thoughts crashing through his head; his expressions changed, from disbelief to horror to grief. He was trying to process what he'd just heard.

Then he slumped in his seat. The tears flowed silently down his cheeks. The others were hushed for several minutes, waiting for Sonny to calm down, waiting for the truth to sink in.

Finally, his sister said, "You served your time. You're out now and free. Don't make any more trouble." She put her hand on his shoulder.

He shook it off. "I'm not free at all! I just killed the wrong woman— I thought it was you!"

Suddenly Sonny jerked away from the men. "I gotta get out of here."

Char nodded to the men to let him go, and Sonny charged for the door. Without missing a beat he picked up a tall Chinese vase and smashed it on the tile. Then he was out the door dashing down the steps.

CHAPTER 28

Char made a nod to the men, requesting them to leave the room.

She turned to Gwen. "May I ask who you are?"

Shaking, Gwen collapsed in a chair. "I knew what he planned to do. He was afraid I'd call the police, so he forced me to come with him."

"How can I help?"

Just then they heard the squeal of wheels which they knew must be Sonny peeling out of there.

"That's my car!" Gwen said.

"Where would you like to go? How can I help?" Char said.

Gwen tried to think. Where would it be safe? Not her apartment, not *The Haven*. Maybe she could go to Eric's for the night.

"May I use your phone?"

"Of course."

With shaking hands she called Eric, told him in as few words as she could that she was in danger and could she stay at his place for the night.

"Where are you?"

"In San Francisco."

"I'll come and get you."

"No, I can call a cab."

"Give me your address."

She didn't have any fight left. "2439 Octavia."

"I'll be there right away."

She returned to the others. "My friend is coming to get me. He lives in Marin. Do you mind my waiting here?"

"Make yourself comfortable. It appears you've gone through quite an ordeal. I'll fix you some tea."

Char had dismissed the men, but feeling they should stay in case the man returned, they had retired to another sitting room.

Gwen closed her eyes, and took some deep breaths. Was it true that this crisis was over? Nothing seemed real to her, not that she was in a brothel, not that the hated sister was about to bring her tea, not that she'd discovered Sonny in the bathtub. The bricks of reality were tumbling down.

The tea came, and with it a plate of paté and crackers.

"I thought you might be hungry."

She hadn't eaten for hours, but she had no appetite for food.

"If you want to talk, I'd be glad to listen," Char said, sitting down.

Gwen didn't feel like repeating the macabre story. Char sensed this, and decided to start the conversation.

"We were close, very close as kids. Did he tell you?"

Gwen nodded.

"He thinks I've put him out of my mind. The truth is, I was kind of expecting this call. I know when he got out of prison. I've been in contact all along with the superintendent of Folsom, tracking his behavior, when he went before the parole board, and so on. Visiting him was impossible, as he, well, he can be very volatile."

Gwen nodded. How well she knew.

"Almost immediately he went into denial and couldn't believe he'd done it. I love my brother, but that night changed everything."

They were silent for a few minutes. Gwen sipped her tea.

"I always felt guilty that it was he who did time," she said. "You see, he was always weak, and depended on me to make decisions for us. That night he was just being a loyal soldier. I'm the one that should have been in prison. I called out 'shoot.' And he did."

Gwen said nothing.

"What good would it have done for me to turn myself in as an accessory? It wouldn't have gotten him out."

Was she looking for someone to agree with her? Gwen said nothing.

"Did he treat you badly?" Char asked.

"Sometimes."

"How well did you know him?"

"This is the second time he captured me."

"I'm so sorry."

"I'm glad to be safe now."

"I should love to know your story."

"Perhaps another time."

"Yes, you're exhausted."

"Do you think he'll come back?"

"To kill me? No. I think he finally realized that it was he who pulled the trigger. He has to come to terms with that. He may even feel some shame for what he was about to do tonight. Maybe someday . . ." She left off in a wistful manner.

When the doorbell rang, Char answered the door and ushered Eric and Denise into the room.

Gwen rose and went to them. She introduced them to Char and thanked her for her hospitality.

When they were leaving, Char said, "Call me anytime."

As they approached the car, Gwen realized this was Denise's car.

"I forgot. You don't have a car, do you, Eric?"

"No. Denise drove me. We're getting to be a rescue team."

"I'm so sorry about all this," Denise said, gesturing to the house, the street, the situation.

"So am I. Thank you."

"Now let's get you out of here."

The three of them sat in the front, crowded on the bench seat.

Eric asked, "Are you OK?"

"I am now."

He took her hand. "How did you get mixed up with him a second time?"

"It's a long story."

They drove onto the bridge—at this wee hour they were the only ones on it. And then continuing on 101, they were the only ones driving north along the dark curves toward Sausalito, with steep hills on their left, and a deep ravine on the right. Suddenly a host of blinking red lights ahead warned them that there'd been an accident.

Gwen put her arm on Denise's. "Stop. Please stop."

"Why?"

"Please."

Denise pulled over several yards beyond the emergency vehicles.

"It could be . . . it might be . . . " She got out of the car and Eric followed her.

A deep gorge lay below the broken steel guard on the road. Eric could see a blaze below. He pulled Gwen toward him. "Don't look."

But she twisted around. Far below she could see a car burning.

"Eric, what kind of car is it?"

"I'll ask the officer."

They walked up to a fireman.

"Has anyone determined the make of the car?"

"It's an old VW."

Gwen caught her breath. "Who was in it?"

The fireman got on his walkie-talkie. "How many casualties?"

She heard the answer. "Just a single man."

That was enough.

Eric thanked the fireman and turned her around. They headed back to the car.

Gwen held herself together on the ride back to Eric's houseboat.

When they were inside she dropped down on the couch and began to sob. Eric sat beside her, and she buried her head in his lap. The sobbing continued for some time, as he did his best to comfort her.

Still sniveling, she sputtered out, "It's just so sad. He wasn't really a bad person."

Eric had his own view on this.

"That one night spoiled his life."

"And ended a couple of others."

She looked up. "Do you think he did it on purpose— going off the cliff?"

He shook his head. "You'll probably never know."

"He was so upset; it could have been an accident— on those curves, in the dark."

"Maybe."

"On the other hand, after finally realizing that he was the one— "

"Shh. Try not to puzzle it out tonight. What you need is a good night's sleep."

She nodded, then to her surprise she yawned.

He brought her a pillow and some blankets.

She made her way to the bathroom. Before she left, she washed her face, and saw how awful and haggard she looked.

When she came back, she said, "I have to call Mark. He'll be worried to death."

"I called him for you, while you were in the head."

"Did he want to come here?"

" He said if you feel safer here tonight, that's OK. He'll come for you in the morning, closer to noon, I hope. I told him you'd need to catch up on your sleep."

"Thank you."

With fits and starts she slept, dreamed and awoke. Once she was still in the car with Sonny as they went through the guard rail, and down, down for miles into a fire pit below. She screamed out loud and Eric came to her side. She hung onto him, shaking as she told him her dream.

"Do you want to sleep in the bed with me? I'll behave myself. Maybe you'd feel safer."

She was tempted, but she declined.

"I'll be OK now."

In the early morning, with light pouring in the window she woke up. Eric was already padding softly around the kitchen.

"I've had enough sleep, and you haven't. So you're going to the bed now."

This time she didn't resist, and slept peacefully for several hours. Finally, hearing men's voices in the other room, she sat up and listened. It was Mark and Eric.

She jumped out of bed, still in her street clothes, and went to Mark. Holding her tightly in his arms, he said, "I'm so glad to have you back."

Eric had filled him in on how Gwen had ended up in a brothel in San Francisco— as much as he knew, and how she hadn't dared go back to *The Haven*.

Gwen could smell bacon, eggs and coffee, and now she was truly hungry. Still shaky, and feeling fragile, she sat down with the men and ate a full breakfast.

Mark was anxious to get all the details from her, but he knew she'd tell him when she was ready. Right now he had to be satisfied that she was safe.

"He'll never bother you again," he said.

That reminded her of her car in the ravine. She turned to Eric. "Have you heard any more about the car?"

"It was yours."

"Sonny is dead?"

"Yes."

She closed her eyes, feeling some strange mixture of re-lief and sorrow.

"He had every chance to start a new life when he got out of prison," Mark said.

Gwen nodded. What monster had he fed and housed in-side himself all those years that denied his own culpability and turned love for his sister into hatred?

"Barbara's going to make it."

"Oh, that's fabulous." And to herself she thought, Sonny would be very glad to know that.

"Yes. She's going to need a lot of re-hab, but she's com-ing along."

"What about Charlene Osmund? Have they figured out whether it was the boyfriend or Sonny?"

"Nothing for sure yet."

Eric excused himself, saying he had to get to work on his latest project.

Mark took Gwen's hand, and said he had a proposition.

"How would you like a new roommate? You shouldn't live alone, Gwen."

"I was thinking that. But now that danger is out of the way— "

"That danger, but there are still a couple of others."

"You mean Dick, and the bull dog neighbor."

"Yes."

"I can't afford to stay there alone, anyway. I guess I'd better advertise."

"Can I make a suggestion?" He was smiling.

She looked at him closely. "You mean you!"

"Yes. Watcha think?"

"Wow. I don't know. It's all so sudden."

"Let's try it out. Starting tonight."

"I guess that would be the practical thing to do," she teased.

"Trial basis, for a week or two. Oh, and I'll pay more than half the rent."

"Then it's a deal."

Later, in her apartment, she told Mark the whole story, starting with her compulsion to find the source of the leak.

"If it wasn't coming from the apartment above the leaking one, I figured it had to be one of its neighbors. The first time I went up the doors were locked. But then I borrowed a key from your desk to enter. I went in the bathroom, and could tell someone was in the tub. I called, but no one answered. I was sure someone had passed out, or worse. So I opened the door— "

"Oh, God."

"And he lunged at me, dragged me into the tub."

"You should never have gone up there alone. What were you thinking?"

Gwen's eyes filled with tears as she lowered her head. "I don't know. I just felt compelled— "

"Next time you have such a compulsion, please take me with you."

She nodded.

"What was he doing there?"

"He couldn't open the glass door; the knob had fallen off. As the water cooled, he kept adding hot, but apparently the drain wasn't working well, and the tub overflowed."

"Did you know who was in there?"

"No, of course not! I would never have opened the glass door. And he knew better than to call for help; he knew I'd recognize his voice. I thought it was someone else who'd passed out, or worse."

"If you're going to play lady detective you're going to have to wise up, Sweetheart."

He took her in his arms and soothed her. "I don't want to lose you."

She enjoyed this comforting for a few moments, and then she said, "About the leak— it must have run down a horizontal beam under that floor and dripped into the apartment below."

"That's what I figured. We had to move the folks in that leaky apartment to another unit. And I've been waiting two days to get a proper plumber."

Gwen nodded.

"He said this Charlene wasn't his sister. He was determined to find his real sister. That's why he was still in the building."

"Eric told me some of this."

And another mystery is solved," she said. "Remember we couldn't figure out how the guy was getting from floor to floor?"

"Yes."

"Guess what? He was riding up and down in the dumb waiter."

"You're kidding!" he said.

"No, it's true."

"How did you figure that out?"

"He made me get in it, when we left the building."

Mark just shook his head in disbelief. Then he looked at his watch.

"Listen, love, I have to go back to work today. We had another death this week, and I have to meet with the family."

"No! Not another— "

"No. This was heart failure."

Gwen sighed in relief. "Do you mind if I go with you?"

"Not at all. But I thought you didn't want to see *The Haven* in your worst dreams."

"I need to see Megan, and I'd like to talk with Lorena again, if that's alright with you."

"Sure, but why?"

"Something's been bothering me since our last talk. I don't think she told me everything. I had the feeling she was holding something back."

"OK."

"Does Megan know I was missing?"

"Yes, rumors got around."

They arrived at *The Haven* shortly before the cleaning ladies' shift ended.

"I'll call Lorena up. You can use my office."

As soon as she got in the building Gwen was surrounded by the girls.

"Where have you been?" demanded Peggy Sue.

"We missed you," said Paula.

"Were you captured?" asked Arlene.

"Someone told us you were dead," said Marjorie. "I'm glad that's not true."

"So am I," said Gwen. She tried to move away.

"And another thing," Peggy Sue said. "Your aunt is seeing an awful lot of that newcomer."

"Did you know that?" Paula said.

"I'm glad to hear it," Gwen said.

"We don't know anything about his character. She should be very careful," Peggy Sue punctuated with a pointed finger.

"He could even be, you know," added Marjorie.

"I'll speak to her," Gwen said, slipping away from them.

When Lorena arrived, again looking frightened, Gwen indicated a chair for her.

"You're not in trouble, Lorena. There are just a few more things we need to know to put this case to bed. You want to help us, don't you?"

Dropping her eyes, Lorena nodded.

"Please tell me anything you might have left out, or forgotten to tell before."

Lorena twisted in her chair and bit her lip. She said nothing.

"There is something else, isn't there?"

Gwen opened a coke, and gave it to the girl.

Lorena took several long sips, before wiping her mouth, and clenching the bottle with both hands.

"You'll feel better if you get it all out. I know you will."

Still the girl said nothing.

Gwen decided to wait patiently until Lorena was ready to talk.

Finally, squirming in her seat, she whispered, "At first I thought she was sleeping, but then, then— she was dead!"

"Miss Osmund was dead?"

Lorena nodded.

"How do you know this?"

"I tried to wake her. I even shook her. Her eyes were open, but she, she— oh it was horrible."

She buried her face in her hands. "I never seen a dead person before. It made me sick. I go to the bathroom and throw up. Then I come back. I pick up the things and put them in the bag and take them down to her locker."

"You were the first person to discover her body?"

She cringed. "I guess so. I didn't kill her, Ma'am. Honest I didn't!"

"No one is accusing you of that."

"I was afraid they'd think I did it."

"No, no. You're in the clear on that score. "Thank you, Lorena. Thank you for telling me this."

"Will I get in trouble? For not reporting it?"

"I don't know, Lorena."

The girl looked so pitiful, that when she rose to leave Gwen gave her a hug.

When Gwen reported the interview to Mark, he said, "Hmm, that doesn't really tell us who the killer was, does it?"

"Sonny told me he did it, said he killed the wrong woman— Charlene Osmund."

"I don't know. It feels like we're back to square one."

"If Lorena is to be believed, I pity her when Ravinski gets his hands on her," Gwen said."

"Yes, withholding that crucial information all this time. Lying. Why do you think she did that?" Mark said.

"I think she was frightened. Afraid we'd think she did it, and afraid she'd get in trouble if she admitted she'd seen the dead body but hadn't reported it."

"And how do we know she's telling the truth now?"

"I think she is."

"I've got to report to Ravinski, and he'll put the heat on the boyfriend. That man's not out of the frying pan yet."

"And I have to see Megan. Maybe we'll have supper together."

Gwen made a wry smile, kissed Mark lightly and made her way upstairs. She knocked and opened the door simultaneously as she was used to doing.

What she saw surprised and embarrassed her. Megan was sitting on the sofa next to the newcomer. They were drinking coffee.

She put her hand to her mouth. "Oh, I'm sorry. I'll just—" She started to back out.

"No, come in, Gwen. I'd like you to meet someone."

Still chagrined, Gwen crossed the living room.

"Sit down, Dear. Mik, I'd like you to meet my niece, Gwen. Gwen, this is Mik McLaughlin.

"Oh, yes, I've heard about you."

Another blunder. She'd made it sound like Megan had been gushing or gossiping.

"Will you have some coffee with us?"

"No, I can't. Mark's expecting me. Sorry I intruded. Really."

She smiled. "I'm glad to have met you," she told Megan's friend.

He rose, and shook her hand. "And I'm so glad to have met you, Gwen. Megan speaks of you often."

As she left, she thought often? How much had they been seeing each other in this short while?

Later in the day, she joined Mark and they drove back to Sausalito. On the way he said, "We'll have to do something about getting you a car."

She'd been thinking of that too. "I'm not sure what to do. I can't really afford another car now."

"You had insurance on the VW, didn't you?"

"Yeah, but only liability."

"Tomorrow, we'll look into it."

"Tomorrow I have to go to work, if I still have a job. I've eaten up all my vacation time on this case. Should I call it a case?"

"That's a good word. And you shall be rewarded."

CHAPTER 29

When Mark dropped her off at work she approached with trepidation the entrance to the bullpen in which she worked. She was greeted as usual by the ever-present cacophony of rattling typewriters. She wore an invisible armor against any crass remarks the horrid Dick would make. After all, if she could survive Sonny and his machinations, she could deal with Dick. No one was sitting at his desk. There was a note on hers.

"Please come to my office, Gwen." It was signed by Martin Vandermere.

Oh, God, had she been away once too often? Was he going to fire her?

She knocked on his door, and he signaled her to come in.

"I'm so sorry. You'll never believe this, but I was kidnapped by the murderer, and made to go to a brothel where he— "

Suddenly she realized how stupid it sounded, like some bodice-ripper tale she'd made up on the way to work.

Martin held his hand up for silence.

"I know, and I can't tell you how it grieves me to think of what you went through."

"How did you know?" she gasped.

"Your friend Mark called me." He smiled. "He told me to go easy on you."

Gwen felt the blood rise to her face.

"I didn't ask you to come in here about your absence. I have good news for you."

Gwen shifted gears. "You do?"

"Your nemesis is gone."

"Dick?"

"The very same."

She wanted to hug him.

"I had to fire him. He had an article printed that I had not OK'd, and didn't approve of. That was the last straw."

Gwen breathed a sigh of relief. "Thank you, so much. That's the best news I've had all week."

~~~

Mark picked her up at five. He had a sparkle in his eye.

"What are you smiling about?"

"Oh, nothing," he teased.

"Tell me."

He only smiled as they drove through the usual rush hour traffic out of the city.

"Is it funny? Is it a joke?"

"No, I wouldn't call it that."

"It makes you happy."

"Yes, it does. And it should make you happy too."

"A gift?"

"Yes."

"A fan!"

"No, sorry."

"Then tell me."

"It's a surprise. You'll have to wait."

Gwen willed herself to be patient. She gave Mark her good news that Dick had been fired."

"Wonderful, finally you'll have him off your back."

They took the first exit after the bridge. How refreshing it was to sit next to the man she loved and have the freedom to look at the Bay and all its boats bobbing on the water, as they followed the twists of the road and headed downhill toward home.

They drove onto Second Street, then up to Third where he parked his car. Mark got out and went around to open the door for her.

"You're grinning," she said.

"And now before you, my dear." He made a dramatic gesture toward the car behind his.

Gwen was puzzled. Did he, no he couldn't mean . . .

"For you, Love."

"Me!" she squealed. She ran to it. "My God, Mark. You didn't. I can't pay you for it."

"You already have. You earned it."

"Oh, not half!"

She ran her hand over the hood of the Hudson. "I can't get over it."

"Slow down. It's not new; it's ten years old, the last year they made Hudsons. But it was driven very little, as Mrs. Nelson had a stroke soon after she bought it. She's recovered, but was advised by her doctor not to drive anymore. It's been sitting in the garage for years."

"Still, how did you get it?"

"I asked her if she'd like to sell it. She would. And she gave me a very good price when she found out who was going to get it."

"I remember her. She came to several meetings, and never complained."

"She's grand. And she wanted to show her appreciation for your calm way of presenting facts, and what a good listener you were. Those are her words."

"But she could get quite a bit more for it."

"Believe me, she doesn't need the money. I took it for a tune-up today, got a new battery, and had it washed and waxed."

When he opened the door for her, she sat on the bench seat caressing the upholstery, then studying the dashboard.

"It's so fine. I can't believe it. Should I say 'You shouldn't have?'"

"Never. You earned it. Come on, now. After dinner we can take it for a spin."

"I want to go now!"

"Alright."

He climbed in the passenger side and handed over the keys. A little blue bow was tied to the key ring.

"It's automatic!" Gwen said.

"That should make it easier for you to stop and start at all those lights in the city."

She turned it on, and was about to drive off, but he said, "Not so fast. There are other things you need to know about any car you haven't driven before. Do you know how to turn the windshield wipers on?"

She considered the options. "No."

Mark showed her how, showed her where the turn signals were, and other necessities for driving.

"Do you know how to open the windows?"

"Even my lowly VW had windows that opened," she laughed.

"Like this?"

Mark pressed a button, and the passenger side window rolled down.

"Oh, God— electric windows," she squealed.

"Nothing but the best."

When she turned the wheel to leave the parking spot, she pulled it too far.

"Gwen, this has automatic steering. Don't work so hard."

"OK."

They drove north through town and onto the freeway. Before long, she was cruising right along.

"Hey, you're way over the speed limit. You don't want a ticket, do you?"

She glanced at the speedometer and slowed down. "I had no idea I was going so fast."

"With a large car, it can fool you."

"Such a smooth ride. Oh, Mark, I love it."

"Aren't you getting hungry? I am. You know, this isn't the last time you can drive. Let's call it a day, until tomorrow."

Reluctantly, Gwen took the next exit and drove back home.

Their love-making had always been good, but that night with the thrill of the new car, and the loss of her nemesis, her energy and enthusiasm were brought to new heights, which in turn, caused Mark to respond with multiple orgasms. They fell asleep still entwined in each other's arms.

~~~

On their next visit to Barbara Kelly's room, they found her quite alert. She was eager to talk.

"I do remember being attacked now. But it all happened so fast. I'm told he knocked me out. I only had a glimpse of him."

"Could you tell us what you remember of this glimpse?"

"He was a few inches taller than I am— maybe five feet ten. And he wore glasses."

"Do you remember any facial features?" Gwen asked.

Barbara shook her head.

Gwen said, "I'm going to show you a picture. I want to know if you recognize this man."

She placed a picture of Sonny on the bed. "Was this the man?"

"Oh, my God!" She covered her mouth in fear.

"You needn't fear him ever again. He's dead."

Gwen was delighted that Barbara was recovering her memory, as well as her speech.

When she reported Barbara's progress to Mark, he said, "I have wonderful news for Barbara. One of the residents started a fund to collect money for her to go to Ireland when she's ready."

"Oh, Mark, that's splendid. Have you told her?"

"The resident who started the fund is going to tell Barbara. We think it might help her get better faster."

"Yes. That's terrific."

CHAPTER 30

Once more Brutus was brought into the interview room at the police station.

Bernard was doing the questioning. He didn't waste any time.

"Charlene Osmund was no relative of yours."

"Ok, we were friends."

"We know you forged the will. We know you can't be relied on to tell the truth. We believe you murdered Miss Osmund."

"I didn't. I didn't know she had money until— "

"That doesn't jibe with you writing the forged will. It's obvious you wanted her money for your film."

"No, I mean we talked about it. Like I said, she was going to finance it."

"She didn't *offer*, did she?"

"I can't remember who brought it up first, but she was really into it— making this film."

"Again, you've changed your story. You desperately wanted to make this film, right?"

"I wouldn't say desperately."

"I would. When she backed out of financing it, you had to find a way to get her money, didn't you?"

"No, I— there was a misunderstanding."

"You didn't just accept her decision, did you?"

"I didn't like it."

Bernard was moving closer to him, leaning over his shoulder. "You more than didn't like it. You were going to do something about it."

"Hey, it wasn't like that."

"What was it like, Peter? How was it like? What did you do when she refused?" Bernard was shouting in his ear.

"I, I told her to think it over."

"And did she?"

"Yeah."

"You went back there?"

"A couple of times."

"And what was her final answer?"

"She still said no."

"You couldn't leave it at that. You didn't just say 'OK' and walk away."

Peter was sobbing. "I don't know."

"What *did* you do, Peter? You tortured her, didn't you? You whipped her hard."

"Hey, that was part of our game. She liked it."

"She liked to be whipped?"

"Yes, she did."

"Just that last night?"

"No, every time."

"A rich older woman who liked to be whipped."

The detective's shouting was causing pain in his ear. "You gotta believe me. She did. It had nothing to do with our movie plans."

"After you whipped her and got her really turned on, did she change her mind, and go along with your plan?"

"No."

"What did you do then?"

Peter was sobbing.

"You smothered her, didn't you?"

Bernard smashed his fist on the table.

"You did, didn't you?"

"No!"

"What did you do?"

"I don't remember!"

"She refused your plan. What did you do before you left her place? Think, Peter, You were furious with her. You'd spent days and nights planning this venture, and she'd said she'd help you. Then she pulled out. She had no right to do that, did she, Peter? What else could you do? You killed her. She had it coming, didn't she Peter?"

"I didn't mean to," Peter sobbed. "It was an accident."

~~~

Before the day was over, Mark and Gwen got word that Peter had confessed. They could hardly believe it.

"I understand Bernard worked him over real good," Ravinski told them. "Broke him down."

Gwen was quiet that evening.

"What's the matter?" Mark asked. "Something wrong?"

"It just seems so ironic. Sonny died believing he'd killed two women, and he didn't kill either one. Charlene was dead before he got there; he killed a dead woman. And Barbara's getting well."

Mark said, "Guess he thought he'd be spending the rest of his life in prison for those murders and that's why he took that dive."

"Plus he realized he really was the one who killed the officer all those years ago. Do you think he went over the cliff on purpose?"

"I do," Mark said. "That's what the state police concluded. No skid marks, no effort to brake."

"He did try to kill Charlene Osmund, though. It's not like he was innocent."

"No, he wasn't innocent. And look what he put you through."

~~~

"You are a marvel," Martin exclaimed. "The identity of the criminal is finally known. And you were certainly a prime figure in bringing this awful business to a close. And speaking of that, if you're willing, I'd like you to work with me to create an article for the paper about the trials of *The Haven* and the people involved."

"What kind of article would it be?"

"A feature piece. First, if you could tell me everything that happened, leaving nothing out. Then we could work together to hone it down, and filter out anything too personal, irrelevant or not in good taste."

"None of it was in good taste."

"I apologize. I didn't mean it that way. We just don't want it to sound inflammatory."

"Yes, I think that would be exciting."

"That is, if you're willing. It all depends on you, Gwen. I don't want to take advantage of the fact that as a central character in this drama, you happen to work for me. On the other hand, if you'd like to contribute to such an exposé, I'd be honored."

"I would. I'd love to."

They spent the rest of the morning compiling the facts as Gwen remembered them. She had a potpourri of feelings as she did this. Partly it was painful to revisit the terror of those days. But she also felt a certain pride that she could contribute to the important conclusion of crimes which had been terrorizing the residents of *The Haven* for weeks.

Martin took her to lunch. It was meant to be a break from this gruesome story, but she found herself telling the more emotional aspects of her experience, until she was almost shaking, and Martin suggested they change the subject.

They both indulged in a hot fudge sundae, both saying it was not on their menu as they were trying to lose weight. Gwen laughed as Martin told her about his first sundae when he was five, how he'd had to share it with his older brother, and was sure that his brother got more than half.

When they returned they continued working on the article, sharpening it, filtering, omitting overly dramatic details, so as to keep the style in the standard of *the Chronicle*.

In the evening Gwen shared her news with Mark.

"That's great!"

In the next couple of days, Gwen worked on the article alone, trimming and tweaking it. When she thought it was the best she could do, she presented it to Martin.

He was so touched by it, she thought she saw tears in his eye.

"Ready to print," he said with a smile. "Terrific, Gwen."

He got out of his seat and gave her a pat on the back.

At home that evening Gwen shared her news with Mark.

"I'm so proud of you, Gwen." He took her in his arms.

"Now for a reward, how about a little trip? Wouldn't that be fun?"

"Oh, I've been away from work so much."

Mark looked imploringly at her.

"OK, I'll ask."

"Well, you do that. North? South? East? West? No, forget West, too wet."

Without hesitation Gwen said, "I'd love to go down the coast, to Big Sur. You can drive."

"So you can watch the views."

"Right. Well, we can take turns driving."

"Have you ever driven on that curvy road, on the edge of the cliff?"

"No, but I'm ready to practice."

Gwen saw his look of horror, and laughed.

She approached her boss nervously.

"I know I've been away a lot. Feel free to say 'No.' My boyfriend bought me a new car, and well, we thought it would be fun for us to take a few days for a little trip down the coast."

"Can't you take a drive on the weekend?"

Gwen looked chagrined.

Martin burst out laughing. "Just kidding, Gwen. Of course, you can. Some nice R&R for both of you."

~~~

Ravinski took all the credit for solving the murders and bringing the case to conclusion. He made sure the Examiner's chief editor published that information.

The Chronicle, of course, made short shrift of his participation. They published two articles, one giving the facts, in straight press style with few embellishments. The other was a long feature article in which Gwen was given full credit with a by-line, offering up the saga from the beginning, the brave composure of the residents during the whole ordeal, the agonized character of the culprit and his final undoing. It was moving, without being sentimental. The article harvested many favorable editorials.

When it was published, Martin said, "By the way, that by-line is for keeps."

~~~

Mark and Gwen took off in the Hudson, first to the quaint and delightful town of Carmel. Then farther south to Big Sur with its magnificent views of the rocky coastline, its sharp curves and switchbacks, each turn giving them another spectacular view of rocky outcroppings and crashing waves.

And while Mark had sat white knuckled, she had safely driven the last fifty miles of this gorgeous, but harrowing road.

Now rolling the power window down on the passenger side, and scooting along the bench seat closer to Mark, Gwen felt a sort of peace and happiness knowing that at last most troubles were behind her. OK, she still had to face a trial for that ludicrous charge of hit and run, but that was small potatoes compared to all the predicaments she'd put behind her.

As Scarlett said, *I'll think about that tomorrow.*

END

www.ingramcontent.com/pod-product-compliance
Lightning Source LLC
Chambersburg PA
CBHW021004120726
47905CB00009B/2851